"I—I'm sorry," Christina gasped, her heart thudding.

All she wanted was to get down off this horse and bury her face in her dog's neck.

"Hang on, it's all right." In one swift movement Seth swung himself to the ground and held up his hands to Christina. "Let's take a break. I'll help you down."

Too relieved to think beyond the moment, she transferred her grip from the saddle horn to Seth's broad shoulders. With his strong arms supporting her, she slid from the saddle and collapsed against him.

"Easy, easy." Seth soothed her with gentle pats as if she were a jittery colt. "Man, you're really shaking. Never meant to scare you like that."

As her breathing slowed, she became all too aware of Seth's firm chest beneath her cheek, along with the steady, reassuring beat of his heart. If she thought her legs would hold her, she ought to put some distance between them. He was her employer, after all. Besides, how many times would he come to her rescue like this before he convinced his grandmother she was unfit for the job?

Award-winning author **Myra Johnson** writes emotionally gripping stories about love, life and faith. She is a two-time finalist for the ACFW Carol Award and winner of the 2005 RWA Golden Heart® Award. Married since 1972, Myra and her husband have two married daughters and seven grandchildren. Although Myra is a native Texan, she and her husband now reside in North Carolina, sharing their home with two pampered rescue dogs.

Books by Myra Johnson

Love Inspired

Rancher for the Holidays
Her Hill Country Cowboy

Her Hill Country Cowboy

Myra Johnson

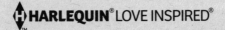

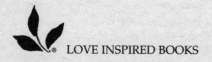 LOVE INSPIRED BOOKS

Recycling programs
for this product may
not exist in your area.

ISBN-13: 978-0-373-62299-3

Her Hill Country Cowboy

www.Harlequin.com

Printed in U.S.A.

Have I not commanded you?
Be strong and courageous. Do not be afraid;
do not be discouraged, for the Lord your God
will be with you wherever you go.
—*Joshua* 1:9

With gratitude for those very special service animals who assist and hearten their humans in so many ways, and with deepest admiration for the dedicated trainers who prepare these animals to serve with loyalty and unconditional love.

Many thanks also to my dear friend and fellow author Janet Dean, whose ideas and insights helped tremendously during the early development of this story. As always, I'm grateful for my family's love and encouragement, as well as the friendship and support of all my "sisters" in Seekerville (seekerville.blogspot.com).

Chapter One

Christina Hunter flexed her stiff fingers gripping the steering wheel and shot an anxious glance at the GPS display on her smartphone. Good, still following the blue line.

"In five hundred feet, turn right."

"Thank you, Map Lady." Flicking on her right blinker, she slowed as she approached the intersection.

Driving through the quaint downtown area of Juniper Bluff, Texas, felt like stepping back in time, but after her near-fatal auto accident two years ago, followed by a slow and difficult recovery, she was more than ready for a change of scenery. Small shops and businesses bordered a central square with a fountain at one end and a gazebo at the other. In the middle stood a statue of a horse and rider. A local hero, maybe? If Christina's new job worked out, she might get to stay long enough to learn something about the guy.

But these days, everything in her life was a big *if*.

After making the turn, Christina patted her sweet, unflappable golden retriever, curled up in the passenger seat. "What do you say, Gracie? Ready to try small-town living?"

The dog thumped her tail, and those big brown eyes, so full of loyalty and affection, tugged hard at Christina's heart.

"I couldn't do this without you, girl. You know that, right—?"

Brake lights ahead jerked Christina's attention back to her driving. A pickup swung over to the curb, and a tall man wearing a cowboy hat jumped out. Trotting to the middle of the road, he waved his arms in a frantic signal for Christina to stop. She slammed on the brakes and thrust out one hand to steady Gracie. Good thing the dog was safely secured in her harness.

Unfortunately, the sudden stop killed the car engine.

Heart pounding, Christina lowered her window and leaned out. "Is there a problem?"

"Sorry," the man yelled. He stooped to pick up something in the street—*a turtle?*—and carried it across to the other side.

"Good grief. Really?" Glancing skyward, Christina shook her head. Was it a thing in small-town Texas to stop and help wildlife safely across the road?

Then she noticed the two anxious faces peering through the rear window of the pickup. A solemn-faced little boy held fast to a smaller girl and patted her shoulder. Even at this distance, Christina could see the girl's chin quivering as she swiped wetness from her cheeks.

Poor kid.

But what a great dad.

Christina's irritation eased. Formerly a social worker who'd championed children in trouble, she'd encountered too many fathers who didn't deserve the title. How could she not admire a man willing to risk life and limb to protect his kids from witnessing a poor, defenseless creature crushed beneath the wheels of an automobile?

On his way back to the pickup, the man caught Christina's eye and tipped his hat, briefly revealing sun-kissed caramel-colored hair in need of a trim. His crooked smile, combined with the happy cheers of his kids as they hung out the driver's-side window, more than made up for the alarm Christina had suffered as a result of her abrupt stop.

Time to settle her nerves and get back on the road so she could meet her new employer. But when she turned the key in the ignition, the only response from under the hood was a rumbling groan. Another try, and the rumble faded to a sputtering cough.

"Not now. Oh, please, not now!" Christina slapped the steering wheel as a fresh surge of anxiety threatened to choke her.

Gracie whined. Rising on her haunches, the dog licked Christina's ear and rested a paw on her thigh.

"I know, I know." Forcing slow, deep breaths, Christina sank her fingers deep into the soft fur behind Gracie's ears.

The man in the cowboy hat appeared at her window. "Everything okay, ma'am?"

"I—I can't get my car started." Christina despised the helpless-female quaver in her voice.

"Pop the hood. I'll take a look."

"That's okay. I can—"

Too late. He'd already moved around to the front of the car. Oh, well, as a newcomer in a strange town, it wasn't as if Christina had a lot of options. A call to the auto club could mean waiting an hour or more, especially this far away from a good-sized city, and she was already a day overdue to start her new job.

Wearily, she found the hood release and pulled the lever. Now all she could see in the space between the dashboard and the hood was the man's strong, capable-looking hands. He fiddled with a car part here, another one there, then told her to try the ignition again.

The car started right up. Christina released a shaky cry of relief as the man slammed down the hood. With an elbow resting on the window frame, she called a relieved "Thank you!"

"No problem. It was kinda my fault, anyway. And thank *you* for stopping." He tilted his head toward the kids watching from the pickup. "If I hadn't rescued that critter, I'd have caught all kinds of what-for from those two."

"Well, we couldn't have that." A pang of envy caught Christina by surprise. Did his wife know how blessed she was to be married to such a caring husband and father? With a quiet sigh, she reached for the gearshift. "I should get going. No more, uh, critters in the road, are there?"

The man looked both ways. "Coast is clear." He hesitated. "You're not from around here, are you?"

Christina attempted a light laugh. "What gave me away?"

"No front license plate. Texas cars and trucks have both front and rear."

Right. And in Arkansas they didn't. Two days on the road and Little Rock already felt like a lifetime ago.

"If you need directions or anything..."

Christina pulled her lower lip between her teeth. She'd been driving almost nonstop since leaving the motel north of Dallas that morning, and she only wanted to reach her destination, meet her new employer and start settling in. Unwilling to risk the GPS getting her lost in the middle of nowhere, she glanced up with a tentative smile. "Maybe you could tell me if I'm heading in the right direction for Serenity Hills Guest Ranch."

One eye narrowed. "You have a reservation?"

"Sort of." It wasn't any of this stranger's business, but her employment arrangement did include the use of a private cabin.

Dipping his head, the man looked past Christina and frowned toward Gracie. "Then you should know the ranch has a no-pets policy."

"Gracie isn't a *pet*. She's a registered service dog." Guess he hadn't noticed the blue vest Gracie wore.

"Be that as it may, you still can't—"

A car horn blared behind them, and Christina startled. In the rearview mirror, she glimpsed a dusty tan SUV.

"Hey, Seth," the whiskered driver bellowed through his open window. "Do your jawin' somewhere's else, will ya?"

"Cool your jets, LeRoy. The lady just had a little car trouble. Pull around if you're in a hurry."

Car trouble she *wouldn't* have had if *Seth* hadn't forced her to stop so he could move a turtle out of danger. And now he was telling her they wouldn't allow Gracie at the ranch? Obviously, he was ignorant about laws regarding service animals.

And obviously, she'd misjudged his solicitous nature.

As the SUV eased around them, Christina gripped the steering wheel and shot a curt glance at the man at her window. "Thanks again for getting my car started. I'm sure I can find my way from here."

"But the dog—"

She didn't give him a chance to finish. Shifting into Drive, she left the do-gooder cowboy and his pickup behind. This transition was hard enough without letting an opinionated—and clearly uninformed—stranger rattle her.

So much for her initial admiration for a kindhearted dad who rescued defenseless animals. She could only pray she didn't cross his path again anytime soon.

Seth Austin ground his teeth. Yes, the guest ranch had been short on business this summer, but the last thing he needed was a lodger who thought she could ignore the rules.

Although he was pretty certain he would have remembered if they'd had a reservation for a Tuesday night. Most of their guests arrived on Thursday or Friday for a weekend stay, or else on Sunday if they had reservations for a full week.

Then it hit him. His grandmother had hired a new housekeeper, who should have reported yesterday, only something had come up and she'd postponed her arrival for a day.

"Please, please, *please*, Lord," Seth mumbled as he strode to his pickup. "Don't let that woman be her."

She sure didn't look like any housekeeper they'd ever had on the place. Too pretty, for one thing—and it galled Seth to realize he'd even noticed. Shoulder-length golden-blond hair, eyes the color of fresh-brewed coffee. And just as potent, apparently, because Seth couldn't feel more wired if he'd polished off a whole pot of his grandmother's strong brew.

"Daddy?" Nine-year-old Joseph scrambled out of the

way as Seth climbed into the cab. "Is the turtle gonna be all right?"

"Sure thing. He's probably happily munching on dandelions by now." Seth twisted around to make sure Eva, his six-year-old, was buckled into her booster seat behind him.

Joseph crawled between the seats and buckled up in his spot next to Eva. "Who was that lady in the car, Daddy?"

"Just somebody new in town."

Eva sniffled. "She had a big dog."

"I know, honey. But it's gone now. Nothing to worry about." Laying his Stetson on the passenger seat, Seth sent his little girl a reassuring smile through the rearview mirror, then belted in behind the wheel. On the worrisome chance the woman *was* the new housekeeper, he'd be sending her right back to town with directions to Doc Ingram's so she could board that beast of hers at Juniper Bluff's only veterinary clinic. Service dog or not, Seth wasn't about to let the animal anywhere near his kids.

He had one more stop to make on his way home. At the farm-and-ranch supply on the outskirts of town, the kids latched onto both his hands as he waited for Wally, the teenage store helper, to load four fifty-pound bags of horse feed into the pickup bed. When Wally tipped his baseball cap at Eva, she scooted farther behind Seth's leg.

"Shy as ever, ain't you, sweet thing?" Wally glanced up at Seth with a regretful frown.

Seth had long ago grown tired of fending off such remarks about his little girl, skittish as a newborn foal. Eva would get over her timidity when she was good and ready. "Thanks, Wally. Hop in the truck, kids."

Twenty minutes later, he backed the pickup up to

the barn door. As he helped the kids to the ground, his grandfather ambled through the opening. Bryan Peterson, Seth's mother's dad, walked with a slight limp, thanks to his horse taking a misstep some twenty years ago and both of them landing in a gully.

The kids darted over to greet their great-grandfather, affectionately known as Opi, a German endearment for *grandpa*. "Daddy helped a turtle get to the other side of the road," Joseph announced. "Then he had to fix a lady's car that wouldn't start."

"Sounds like y'all had yourselves a little adventure in town." Opi tousled Joseph's mop of tawny hair. "Why don't you take your sister to the house? I think Omi has some chocolate chip cookies fresh from the oven."

Seth's heart clenched as he watched the indecision play across his son's face. Since their mother's death not quite three years ago, neither of the kids strayed far from Seth's side. But the lure of those fresh-baked cookies finally won out. Joseph grabbed Eva's hand, and together they jogged across the lane to the white three-story farmhouse that served as both their home and the guest ranch offices.

Only then did Seth notice the blue compact sedan parked in the gravel lot behind the house. He yanked off his Stetson and slapped it against his leg. "Shoulda known."

"What, son?" Opi hefted one of the feed sacks.

"The car over there. Our new housekeeper?"

"Yep. Pretty little thing." As if Seth needed reminding. "Your grandma's getting her paperwork in order." Shifting the feed sack to his shoulder, Opi started for the storeroom.

"You told her she couldn't keep the dog here, right?"

"It's a service dog. Got no choice."

Bile rose in Seth's throat. They most certainly did have a choice. Omi would just have to find another house-keeper.

He stormed across the lane, but before he made it to the back door, he spied Eva shivering on the wooden swing at the far end of the porch. "Aw, baby."

She pulled her thumb out of her mouth long enough to whimper, "The big dog's in there, Daddy!"

"It's okay, it's okay." Sweeping Eva into his arms, he sank onto the swing and held her close. It was all he could do to speak calm, soothing words to his little girl while a cauldron of fury boiled in his gut.

"Omi gave me a cookie and said to wait out here." Eva looked up, tears pooling in eyes as brown as the choco-late smearing the tip of her nose. "Can you make the big dog go away?"

Seth fully intended to, but he dare not make promises to his daughter until after he cleared the matter with his grandmother. Marie Peterson pretty much ruled the roost at Serenity Hills Guest Ranch, and she'd have to be the one to send this woman on her way.

"Tell you what," he said, shifting Eva onto the swing beside him. "I'll walk you over to Opi in the barn, and you can give him a hand feeding the horses while I talk to Omi about the lady with the big dog."

The suggestion seemed to mollify Eva. She nodded and slid off the swing, then clung to Seth's fingers as they headed over to the barn. Once Eva had transferred her death grip from Seth's hand to Opi's, Seth marched back to the house. He squared his shoulders and hauled in a determined breath before yanking open the screen door.

Stepping into the kitchen, he found Joseph perched

on a barstool at one end of the granite counter. A milk mustache adorned the boy's upper lip, and cookie crumbs dotted the counter. At the oak trestle table beyond, the housekeeper wannabe sat with her back toward Seth while Omi went over some paperwork with her. The dog lay on the floor between their chairs.

Joseph didn't share Eva's intense fear of dogs, but he still looked plenty glad to see his dad walk in. He jumped down and ran over to hug Seth around the waist. "Where's Eva?"

"With Opi." Seth kept his voice light. "You want to go help them in the barn?"

Joseph's welcoming smile faded. "Can't I stay here with you?"

"I need to talk business with Omi. Go keep an eye on your sister, okay?"

Lower lip thrust out, Joseph trudged across the kitchen. Seth waited until he heard the back door bang shut, then strode around the bar.

Omi looked up as he approached. "Hey, Seth, meet our new housekeeper. Christina, this is my grandson, Seth Austin."

He glared at the woman while trying to ignore how her hair shimmered beneath the wagon-wheel chandelier. "I believe we've already met."

Her pulse skittering, Christina looked up with a gasp. "You?"

"Surprise." Seth Austin's greeting held no warmth whatsoever.

"Seth...?" Mrs. Peterson's tone was part question, part warning.

"We sort of ran into each other in town this afternoon," Seth muttered. He looked pointedly at Gracie. "I told you we can't have dogs on the place."

"We've already talked this through," Mrs. Peterson said patiently. "Gracie is Christina's service dog."

"Yeah, I got that." Seth's fierce stare wavered as he glanced toward his grandmother. "But think about Eva. You know this can't work." He swung his gaze back to Christina. "I'm sorry, Miss—"

"Hunter." Christina swallowed nervously. Was she about to get fired before she'd even filled out her W-4?

"Miss Hunter. Like I told you in town, we've got rules. This is a working ranch, and safety is our number one concern. We aren't in a position to start making exceptions."

Whining softly, Gracie sat up and rested her chin on Christina's leg. When Christina glanced down into those soft, expressive eyes, the tension that had welled at Seth's arrival slowly subsided. One hand on Gracie's head, she sat a little straighter and cleared her throat. "I don't think you understand, Mr. Austin. As long as Gracie isn't disruptive and doesn't interfere with my work, I have the legal right to keep her with me."

Jaw clenched, Seth backed up a step. His steely gaze combed Christina from head to toe. "Housekeeping at a guest ranch isn't exactly light work, and you look pretty able-bodied to me." His tone turned skeptical. "So forgive me for asking, but what exactly is your disability?"

Christina pressed her lips together. She should be used to the question by now, along with the typical doubts. If she'd lost her sight or hearing, or if she were in a wheelchair, her disability and need for a service animal would be obvious. But when she explained she'd suffered a brain injury and had post-traumatic stress disorder, she'd come to expect the raised eyebrows and dubious frowns.

Before she could form a response, Mrs. Peterson interrupted. "Now, Seth, stop the third degree and be a gentleman. Christina's been forthright with me about why she needs Gracie, and I'm not anticipating any problems."

Seth glared at his grandmother as if debating his chances of winning this argument. Christina held her breath and prayed. She needed this job. It could mean the difference between being stuck forever living with her overprotective parents or groping her way back to independence and a normal life.

"All right, have it your way." With a sharp exhalation, Seth turned to go. Before he'd taken three steps, he swung around and leveled a finger at Christina. "But first sign of a problem and you're out of here, got it? And keep that dog away from my kids."

Christina didn't realize how badly she'd started shaking until she felt Gracie's wet nose beneath her palm. Giving the dog all her attention, she forced herself to breathe. *Get back in the car and go home*, her inner voice demanded. *You're not ready. This was a mistake. A huge, horrible mistake.*

Mrs. Peterson set a glass of water at Christina's place. "Seth's all bluster and very little bite. He's got his issues, too. Give him time and he'll come around."

After taking a sip of water, Christina slid the employment papers across the table. "You've been very understanding, but your grandson clearly doesn't want me here." She pushed unsteadily to her feet. "I don't think this is going to work out after all."

"Now hold on, honey." Mrs. Peterson shoved the paperwork back toward Christina. "We've got fourteen guests coming for a family reunion this weekend. Where do you think we're gonna find another housekeeper on such short notice?"

Christina sighed and glanced toward the window. Near the barn, Seth knelt in front of his children, and the little girl's face looked anything but happy. When she and her brother had come to the house earlier, the girl had taken one look at Gracie and run screaming into her great-grandmother's arms. At least Mrs. Peterson hadn't over-reacted. She'd calmly offered the little girl a cookie and led her out to the porch.

Seth had issues? Apparently his children did, too. As an experienced child and family social worker, and emotionally traumatized herself as a result of her auto accident, Christina recognized the signs. Was it possible God had sent her here for this very reason, to offer help to a troubled family?

Shoulders sagging, she returned to her chair. "All right, I'll stay. But let's take it one day at a time. The last thing I want is to cause more problems for those kids."

"Believe me, honey, you'll be like a breath of fresh air around here. I felt it in my bones from our very first phone interview." Mrs. Peterson handed Christina a pen. "Let's get these papers filled out, and then I'll show you to your cabin so you and Gracie can get comfortable in your new digs."

Chapter Two

Seth kept the kids occupied helping Opi with simple barn chores until he was certain their new housekeeper had finished her business with Omi and had gone to her cabin. He couldn't avoid Christina Hunter indefinitely, but he'd make sure she kept her dog well away from Eva. This being Christina's first night on the place, Seth figured Omi would invite her to the house for supper, so he decided to take the kids down to the picnic area by the lake and grill something for just the three of them.

While he stood in the utility room digging through the chest-type freezer for franks or burgers, Omi came up behind him. "I know you're mad, Seth, but you might as well get over it. Christina's staying. And so is her dog."

He nearly rammed his head on the freezer lid as he straightened to face his grandmother. "I don't tell you how to run the ranch, so I'd appreciate it if you didn't interfere in how I take care of my kids."

"That's a laugh!" Omi set her hands at her ample waist. "You've always got plenty to say about how we run things around here, and I'm right glad you do. But the truth is, somebody *needs* to tell you a thing or two about how you're raising those youngsters. Georgia's been gone three years now. You aren't helping your kids one bit by mollycoddling them like you do."

"You know as well as I do the heartache Joseph and Eva have suffered." Seth fought to keep his voice level. "I'm just trying to give them the room they need to heal. What's wrong with that?"

"Not a blasted thing. Except I worry all this *room* you're giving them—without the benefit of some kind of counseling—is just more space to wallow in their grief and fear."

"We tried counseling." Returning his attention to his quest, Seth pushed aside some frozen pizzas. "If you remember, it was an interfering social worker who nearly lost me my kids."

"You can't write off the whole field of psychology because one dimwit couldn't see past the end of her nose."

Green beans, stir-fry mix, brown-and-serve rolls—there had to be franks and buns in here somewhere. Seth's fingers were getting numb.

"What exactly are you looking for?" Omi snapped. When he told her his intentions, she scoffed. "No cause to run off and hide. Christina's worn out from her trip. I'm sending a plate of food to her cabin."

Nose in the air, Omi marched out of the utility room, leaving Seth to stew in his own lousy mood. Maybe he had grown too protective of his kids, but he wasn't taking any more chances with their frail little spirits. When Georgia had left him, taking the kids with her, Seth had nearly gone off the deep end. To this day, he couldn't understand why he hadn't been able to make his wife happy right here on the ranch.

But no, with a degree in urban design from Texas

A&M, Georgia wanted more than Juniper Bluff had to offer. When a big-name architectural firm in Minneapolis offered her a position, she said yes first and informed Seth after the fact.

He should have seen right then that there were more problems in his marriage than Georgia's need for career fulfillment.

And he should never have allowed her to take the kids. *He* could shoulder the blame for the upheaval they'd suffered, because if he'd swallowed his stupid male pride and followed Georgia to Minneapolis instead of staying put and waging the war for his marriage and his kids long distance, things might have turned out a whole lot differently.

Some things, anyway. A deep, throbbing ache rolled through him. He slammed down the freezer lid and leaned hard into it while he tried to shove the memories from his mind. The phone call from his mother-in-law saying Georgia had gotten sick. The unbearable wait for test results. The wondering, the questions, the prayers. Then the devastating cancer diagnosis that gave Georgia only weeks to live.

"Seth?" His grandfather's voice sounded behind him. "You okay?"

He straightened and drew a hand down his face. The day's growth of whiskers rasped beneath his palm. "Yeah, fine."

"Omi's got supper on the table. I had the kids wash up."

"Be right there. I need to wash up, too."

A splash of cold water soothed his stinging eyes. Joining his family at the table, he plucked a piece of straw from Eva's hair as he sat down beside her. Leaning over to plant a kiss on her sweet blond head, he thought his heart would burst with all the love he felt for this child. For both his children.

Clearing his throat meaningfully, Opi reached for Eva's hand on one side and Joseph's on the other. Seth joined hands with Eva and Omi as his grandfather bowed his head to offer thanks.

Afterward, Joseph helped himself to a hefty serving of Omi's seasoned pan fries. "Opi says tomorrow we can ride over to Mr. Nesbit's farm and see his calves."

Eva tugged on Seth's sleeve and whispered, "You'll come, too, won't you, Daddy?"

"Sure, hon. Soon as chores are done, we'll all go." It would be a good excuse to get the kids away from the ranch and avoid running into the housekeeper and her dog.

Omi passed a platter of sliced ham to Seth, but before he could serve himself, a knock sounded on the back door. Omi offered a placid smile. "Seth, would you mind?"

He did mind, because the only other person on the place tonight was Christina Hunter. He forked a slab of ham onto his plate and smiled right back. "Maybe you should get it."

"You'll get there faster than I can. Let's not keep our visitor waiting."

Yep, Marie Peterson definitely reigned supreme at Serenity Hills. Muttering under his breath, Seth wadded his napkin next to his plate and marched to the door. Through the glass pane, he glimpsed Christina standing on the porch, arms folded as she glanced right and left. The evening dusk was gathering, and something about the anxious look on her face made him swallow the caustic greeting on the tip of his tongue.

He opened the inner door and spoke through the screen. "Can I help you?"

"Oh. Hi." She seemed surprised to see him standing there. "I—well—this is embarrassing, but I've already locked myself out of my cabin."

"Hang on. I'll get you another key." Seth should have invited her inside, but it wasn't happening while she had the dog with her. He slipped down the short hallway to the office, where he fetched a duplicate key.

On his return trip, his grandmother stopped him in the kitchen and handed him a tray covered with an oversize checkered napkin. "Here's Christina's supper. Tell her to come on over for breakfast in the morning, seven sharp."

Seth ground his teeth. Good thing the kids rarely came downstairs before seven thirty. "You planning on having her eat with us every meal?"

"Of course not. Just till she settles in and has a chance to pick up some groceries for herself."

Lips in a twist, Seth dropped the key onto the tray and continued to the back door. He nudged it open with his hip. "My grandmother sent this tray for you. The key's right here."

"Thanks. Sorry to cause so much trouble." One hand on the dog's head, Christina looked ready to jump out of her skin.

Seth figured he'd kick himself later, but his kindlier instincts kicked in. Nice to realize he still had a few. "Would you feel better if I walked you back to the cabin?"

"Please don't bother. You already think little enough of me." Her throat shifted. She reached for the tray. "I'll just—"

"No, wait." Rats, all he needed was to go soft over a woman in distress. Looked like his own supper would be getting cold. "The path can be tricky after dark, especially before all the vapor lights power up. I'll make sure you get back safely."

"You really don't mind?"

Seth harrumphed. "Need to make sure the pasture gates got latched. Might as well see you to your cabin on the way."

Christina looked at him sideways as if she didn't quite believe him, but a little of her apprehension seemed to have lifted. They started down the path together, Seth carrying the tray and making sure to walk on the opposite side from her dog. No sense giving Christina the idea he'd softened his stance on the animal's presence. Because he hadn't and he wouldn't.

The ranch had two staff cabins, located on the far side of the main house and secluded from the guest cabins. They had to walk past the garage and a couple of outbuildings, then through a copse of trees, and Christina kept her hand on the dog's shoulder the whole way. Seth still hadn't been told what her disability was that required a service animal, but if it caused this much anxiety, he could see why the shadowy trek to her cabin might be a problem.

All the more reason she didn't belong on the ranch. He hoped it wouldn't take long for his grandmother to come to the same conclusion, as well.

Christina was glad the cabin's porch light operated on a sensor. The sun hadn't quite set when she'd gone out earlier on a walk with Gracie. Stupidly, she hadn't thought to take her key and discovered too late that the door locked automatically. She'd really, really hoped it would be Mrs. Peterson who answered her knock. Seeing Seth on the other side of the screen door had sent her misgivings soaring. How would she endure working here when his dislike was so palpable?

Except he was being pretty nice at the moment, and it didn't help her nerves one bit now that she knew he was single. Mrs. Peterson hadn't said much about Seth's wife except that they'd separated and soon afterward she'd become ill and passed away.

He set the tray of food on one of the retro-style red metal porch chairs, then picked up the key and unlocked her door. "There you go. Need anything else?"

"I should be fine now. Thank you so much."

"Oh, uh, breakfast at the house at seven. Omi's orders." He even smiled a tiny bit when he said it.

"Omi. What a cute name." Tray in hand, Christina stood in the doorway. "Does it have special meaning?"

"It's a German-family thing. My great-great-grandparents emigrated from Germany and settled in the Fredericksburg area."

"I came through Fredericksburg on my way to Juniper Bluff. Looks like a fun town to visit."

"Yeah." Seth shifted, the need to escape evident in his darting eyes.

"Well. Thanks again." Christina nodded toward the tray, then smiled up at him. "And thank your grandmother for the meal."

He tipped an imaginary hat before retreating down the steps and disappearing into the trees.

With darkness rapidly closing in around the cabin, Christina once again succumbed to doubts. Until last night at the motel, she hadn't been alone overnight since before the automobile accident. The whole time she'd been in the hospital, her mother hadn't left her side except to shower, change clothes and eat. Not that Christina had been aware the first few weeks while she'd lain in a coma, but later, as she recovered, her father had confirmed her suspicions.

Then five months in a rehabilitation hospital, where Christina had a talkative teenage roommate for the first several weeks, then a nosy grandmotherly type for the remainder of her stay. The past year and a half, she'd lived at home with her parents. And Gracie, of course. Christina blessed the day the service dog had come into her life. Gracie's training included sensing Christina's agitation whenever memories of the accident intruded or something else triggered an anxiety attack. A nudge with a wet nose would remind Christina to breathe again and to focus on the present, not the unchangeable past or the uncertain future.

Like now. As Christina sat at the small table in the kitchenette, Gracie's soft whine alerted her to the fact that she'd scarcely eaten half of the delicious meal Mrs. Peterson had sent over. She tore off a piece of ham and offered it to the dog, who happily gobbled it down.

Concentrating on the tasty supper and Mrs. Peterson's kindness helped Christina put the stress of the day behind her. After washing the dishes and stacking them on the tray to return in the morning, she unpacked a few things and arranged her daily medications in the bathroom medicine cabinet. She didn't like having to depend on prescription meds and prayed the day would come when all these drugs for depression, anxiety and migraines would no longer be necessary.

She swallowed her nighttime pills, then changed into her pajamas and propped herself up in bed with the novel she'd brought along. Gracie hopped up beside her and snuggled in close, laying her head on Christina's knee.

Before Christina had read two pages, her cell phone rang. Recognizing the chime she'd assigned to her mother, she snatched the phone off the nightstand. "Hi, Mom."

"I've been waiting to hear from you." Her mother couldn't disguise a note of worry. "Where are you? Did you get there okay?"

"All tucked into my cozy little cabin. A day late, but I'm safely here."

"I was worried after you called from the motel last night. You sounded so frazzled."

"I told you, it was just travel stress. You were right—I had no business trying to drive straight through in one day."

"Well, I'm glad you had sense enough to stop for the night and get some rest." Mom sighed through the phone. "Honey, are you sure you're doing the right thing?"

Gracie crept closer and nuzzled Christina's arm. Her expressive eyes seemed to say, *You're fine. I'm here. Just breathe.*

"Mom, I told you, I *need* to do this. Yes, it's going to be hard, but I've got to start depending on myself again."

"But you could have done so right here in Little Rock, with Dad and me close by if you needed us."

Christina combed her fingers through Gracie's thick coat and sought the words to help her mother understand. "I love you, Mom. And I can never, ever thank you and Dad enough for how you've been there for me every step of the way. But if I'd stayed in Little Rock, it would be too easy to fall back on your support when any little thing went wrong."

"Is that such a bad thing?"

"No, of course not. But I wouldn't be getting better. I need to get stronger, Mom." Tears pricked Christina's eyes. "And I need you to help me by giving me the space to do it."

Her mother grew silent for a moment. "Are you telling me not to call? Not even to find out how you're doing?"

Swallowing hard, Christina squeezed her eyes shut. "Just for a while, okay? I promise I'll call you in a few days, after I've had a chance to learn my new job and…" She started to say, *see if this is going to work*, but that would only play into her mother's concerns, not to mention feed her own.

"Chrissy…"

"I'm really tired, Mom, and I'll be getting an early start in the morning, so I need to go." Christina forced a smile into her voice. "Give Dad a hug for me. Love you both. Bye!"

She clicked off before her mother could wheedle another minute or two of conversation out of her. It was barely past eight, but two days on the road had taken their toll. After slipping on a robe and slippers and tucking the cabin key securely into her pocket, she took Gracie outside for one more trip before lights-out.

As she looked up into the night sky, a gasp caught in her throat. Never in her life had she seen so many stars! The words of a psalm bloomed in her thoughts and swelled her heart: *The heavens declare the glory of God; the skies proclaim the work of His hands.*

She could do this. With God's help, she'd get back into life and once again stand on her own two feet.

By noon the next day, those feet Christina was so insistent on standing on hurt like crazy. She'd trekked from the main house to the storage building to cabin after cabin with Marie Peterson.

Marie's first request, gently worded but firm, was that Gracie remain outside the guest cabins, the public rooms in the main house and the kitchen food-preparation area. "Well-groomed and obedient as Gracie is," Marie stated, "we have to abide by health department regulations and can't risk complaints about dog hair or allergy issues."

Christina understood perfectly, and at each cabin she asked Gracie to stay outside by the door. It was enough to know the dog waited nearby.

Learning what her housekeeping duties consisted of, where supplies were kept and how to find her way around the ranch had taken most of the morning. And not once had she caught a glimpse of Seth Austin. Since his macho-looking maroon truck was nowhere to be seen either, Christina guessed he'd gone off somewhere with his children and was intentionally avoiding her.

"So the soiled sheets and towels go in this bin," Marie said as they stood in the workroom behind the garage. "And then a service picks them up once or twice a week as needed and delivers a fresh batch."

"Got it." Jotting the instructions in her pocket-size notebook, Christina glanced longingly at a metal folding chair propped against the wall. "You said you aren't expecting guests until the weekend, right?"

"They'll start trickling in sometime tomorrow, but most won't arrive till Friday afternoon. You'll need to tidy their cabins each day while they're at meals or out on excursions or whatever."

Good, she needn't worry about too many personal encounters, one huge reason why she'd initially thought this housekeeping position might be something she could handle.

What she hadn't weighed into the equation was the amount of physical labor involved. Pushing a fully loaded maid's cart from cabin to cabin would require the use of muscles Christina hadn't called upon in longer than she cared to admit. At home, her parents paid for biweekly maid service, which had made it easy to grow lazy about everyday household chores. Mom's hovering hadn't helped, and she wouldn't accept that babying Christina so much only prolonged her recovery.

Marie scanned her notes on a clipboard. "That about covers it. Ready for some lunch?"

"Starved!" Christina tucked away her notebook, already overflowing with the lists and reminders she relied upon daily, and fell in step with her employer on the path to the house. "I'm planning on picking up some groceries this afternoon, though."

"No hurry. You're welcome at our table anytime."

"Thanks, but…" Christina's voice faded as she caught sight of Seth leading a horse out of the barn. He moved with the same easy grace she'd observed yesterday when he'd carried the turtle across the road.

"Oh, good, Seth's back." Marie climbed the porch steps and yanked the cord of a big iron bell hanging from the eaves. The sharp clang made both Christina and Gracie jump. "Sorry," Marie said with a chuckle. "Better get used to the sound of the dinner bell."

Seth glanced their way and waved, but when he met Christina's gaze, his smile stiffened and he abruptly turned away.

Following Marie inside, Christina said, "Maybe I should just take a sandwich back to my cabin."

"Nonsense. We're still getting acquainted." Marie pointed through a door off the kitchen. "Powder room's that way. Go wash up, and then you can help set the table."

Clearly, no one argued with Marie Peterson. Besides, it was refreshing not to be pampered.

Hands washed, Christina returned to the kitchen with Gracie ambling alongside. Christina didn't see Marie anywhere, but Seth stood at the counter, a jar of mayonnaise in one hand and a knife in the other.

A scuffling sound to Christina's right alerted her to Seth's little girl clambering up the farthest barstool. Stark terror widened Eva's eyes as she stared at Gracie. "Daddy, the doggy's in here!"

The look Seth shot Christina cut deeper than a knife ever could. "I told you to keep your dog away from my kids."

"I—I'm sorry." Hands trembling, she groped for Gracie's collar, prepared to make a hasty exit.

Gracie had different ideas. The dog plopped down on her haunches and refused to budge.

"Come on, girl. Let's go outside, okay?" Christina flicked a nervous glance at Seth.

He smirked. "I thought service dogs were supposed to be well trained."

"She is. I don't know what's wrong."

Now the dog lay sprawled across the tile floor at the end of the bar. Her mouth opened wide in a yawn, then she rested her chin on her paws and her eyes drifted shut.

"Gracie! What are you doing?" Christina knelt and lifted the dog's head. "Are you okay?"

Gracie responded by swiping her tongue across Christina's nose. Nothing in those bright eyes suggested illness. In fact, Christina had the sudden suspicion that Gracie knew exactly what she was doing.

From the far side of the room came a tiny voice: "Daddy, is the doggy sick?"

"Not sure, sweetie." Two scuffed boot toes appeared at Christina's left. "What's going on with your dog?"

"I don't know. She's never acted like this before." Sitting on her heels, Christina looked up with a helpless shrug.

Marie returned through the door leading to the reception area. "Oh my, is your dog hurt?"

Just as quickly as she'd lain down, Gracie scrambled to her feet. Tail wagging, she trotted over and licked Marie's hand.

Eva whimpered. "Omi, don't let it bite you!"

"Oh, she's fine, honey." Marie gave the dog a scratch behind the ears. "Hey there, sweet thing. Are we friends now?"

Pushing up from the floor, Christina edged away from Seth, who looked ready to charge to his little girl's defense. But Eva's expression, though still fearful, now held a glimmer of curiosity.

Social worker instincts kicking in, Christina saw an opportunity. "Eva, I think Gracie may be a little bit scared, too."

The child's lower lip trembled. "Why?"

"Well, we're both new here, and we both want very much to fit in. She'd be very sad if she thought you didn't like her." Christina scooted one of the barstools closer to Eva's and climbed on so that they were both looking toward Gracie. The dog now sat quietly at Marie's feet.

Marie cast Christina a knowing smile as she knelt and continued stroking Gracie's head. "We like you just fine, Gracie, so don't be scared. You're a good dog, aren't you?"

"But she's so big." Eva's hand crept into Christina's, and her voice fell to a quavering whisper. "I'm scared of big dogs."

Such great fear in such a little girl—it broke Christina's heart. Eva reminded her so much of another little girl, a child who had good reason to be terrified of her abusive father. A child Christina had tried so hard to protect.

And nearly failed.

The blast of a horn. Screeching brakes. The explosive crunch of metal against metal.

As calmly as she could, Christina slid off the bar-stool and prayed her legs would hold her. "Gracie, let's go." This time, her tone left no room for the dog's dis-obedience. "Please excuse me. I—I'll get something to eat later."

Before anyone could stop her, she bolted for the back door and hoped she'd make it to her cabin before she completely fell apart.

The look on Christina's face as she barged out brought a twinge of guilt to Seth's gut. Why he should feel guilty he had no clue. Everything he did was for the sake of his kids, and if this new housekeeper couldn't see how her dog terrified his daughter, then it was her problem, not his.

Opi and Joseph came in shortly afterward, oblivious to the previous goings-on. Omi took over the sandwich fixings, and a few minutes later they sat down for lunch. Though no one talked much while they ate, the disgrun-tled frowns Omi flashed Seth's way left little doubt as to the direction of her thoughts.

Later, with Eva down for a nap and Joseph stretched

out on the family room sofa with a favorite book on his e-reader, Omi informed Seth she needed to talk over some business matters with him in the office.

He didn't need his imagination to guess what "business" his grandmother had in mind.

"Sit down, son." She motioned toward one of two leather barrel chairs in front of the massive mahogany desk. Seth obeyed, and she took the chair opposite his.

He drummed his fingers on his thighs. "If this is about Christina—"

"Actually, it's about *you*. Your attitude isn't cutting it, mister. I won't tolerate you being rude to that sweet girl."

"Omi—"

She silenced him with an upraised hand. "You think I didn't notice those ice-dagger glances you were shooting her way? You've got to give Christina a chance, son. You know what the Bible says about judging people."

"'For in the same way you judge others, you will be judged, and with the measure you use, it will be measured to you.' Yeah, I know. You've quoted the verse so many times I know it by heart."

"Then heed it." Omi sat forward, her gaze earnest. "Seth, honey, I know full well the pain you've suffered. But you don't have a corner on suffering. Grant Christina the benefit of the doubt and stop giving her such a hard time."

Okay, so he'd been a little tough on the woman, but only because of the dog she couldn't seem to go anywhere without. Controlling his tone, he said, "Can you at least tell me *why* she needs a service dog? Because I'm just not seeing it."

Omi sat back with a tired sigh. "All I'll say is that she was in a bad car wreck a couple of years ago. She suffered severe head trauma, among other things. Her disability is post-traumatic stress disorder, along with the lingering effects of the brain injury. Gracie helps keep her on an even keel."

Swiveling toward the window, Seth silently berated himself for being so insensitive. Omi was right—he'd been too quick to judge. "I'm sorry for what she's been through," he said through tight lips. "But she still has to respect my need to protect my kids."

"She does. More than you know."

Seth swung around to face his grandmother. "What's that supposed to mean?"

She merely shook her head as she rose and moved behind the desk. "Tomorrow will be here before we know it. Best get back to work."

When it was clear his grandmother would say nothing more, Seth stood and marched out of the office. He had plenty to do—tack to clean, a pasture gate to repair, a low spot to fill where the horseback-riding trail cut across a creek. Maybe a few hours of hard labor would take the edge off the bitterness that followed him around like his own personal dark cloud.

Later, returning from spreading a load of gravel at the creek crossing, he glimpsed Christina's little blue car turning down the lane to her cabin. His next stop was the broken pasture gate, which meant he'd be working only a scant distance from Christina's door. After parking by the gate, he grabbed his toolbox from the pickup bed and hoped the housekeeper wouldn't decide to walk her dog anytime soon.

While he searched for a replacement bolt for the gate hinge, the cabin door opened. One hand pressed hard against her left hip, Christina trudged to her car. She popped the trunk and leaned inside, then straightened with plastic grocery bags in each hand. With a grimace and a hitch in her step, she started for the cabin.

Go help her, you idiot. The voice inside Seth's head shouted with the volume of a megaphone.

Muttering a few choice words, he slammed down the toolbox lid and strode up the lane. Wedging a neighborly smile into his tone, he called, "Looks like you could use a hand."

Christina halted on the porch steps, her head snapping around in surprise. "Thanks, but I've got it."

The dog stepped between Christina and Seth, not menacingly but clearly sending a message: *Don't mess with my mistress.*

Keeping a respectful distance, Seth firmed his jaw. "You look like you're hurting. Sure you're okay?"

"Fine. Just a little sore." Christina nodded toward the open cabin door. "Excuse me, but these bags are getting heavy, and I've got groceries to put away." When she lifted her left foot, pain slashed across her face. One of the grocery sacks slipped from her grasp.

Seth charged up the steps. With one arm bracing her around the waist, he relieved her of the other bag. "Let's get you inside. You need to sit down."

"I told you, I'm fine." She made a feeble attempt to pull away. "It's just a muscle spasm. I get them from time to time when I overdo."

"Like biting off more than you can chew with a heavy-duty housekeeping job?" Shooting a glance skyward, Seth ushered her inside. He needed to let go of her quickly, because he hadn't held a woman this close since Georgia, and look where that had gotten him. Gently, he eased her into one of the padded side chairs in the sitting area.

She sank down with a groan. "I need time to adjust, that's all. I haven't done anything quite so…" She clamped her mouth shut and reached out for the dog, now poised beside her chair.

After gathering up the grocery bags and depositing them on the kitchen table, Seth planted himself in front of Christina and crossed his arms. "My grandmother explained about your accident. And why you need your service dog."

Christina cast him an uneasy glance. "What exactly did she tell you?"

"Just that you were hurt pretty bad and now you have PTSD." Exhaling sharply, Seth propped a hip on the arm of the chair across from her. "Look, I know we got off to a rough start, and I should probably apologize."

"Probably?" Christina released a shaky laugh.

"Okay, I definitely owe you an apology." He brushed a hand across his nape while deciding how much of his own past to open up about. As little as possible, he reasoned. Doubtful she'd stick around long enough for it to matter. "My grandmother has accused me more than once of being overprotective of my kids."

Was that a smirk on her face? No, more like a smile of acknowledgment. "Yes, I recognized the signs."

"Maybe I am," he said defensively, "but I've got my reasons."

"It doesn't take a genius to figure out your little girl is deathly afraid of dogs." Christina's gaze held his, her tone softening. "May I ask what happened?"

This much he could reveal without too great a risk of deepening the gash in his heart. "My brother-in-law has two Rottweilers. My…wife—" Okay, this was hurting a little more than he'd planned on. He took a stuttering breath. "She, uh, took the kids to visit her brother, and the dogs got a little rough with Eva. She wasn't even three years old then. The dogs each outweighed her by a hundred pounds."

"Oh, no. Was she hurt?"

"A few bruises, and a split lip from being knocked down. It wasn't like they attacked her. They were just being playful and didn't know their own strength."

"Still, she must have been terrified." One hand caressing her dog's head, Christina sat forward. "I promise you, nothing like that will ever happen with Gracie. There isn't a gentler animal alive."

Seth stood. "Just keep her away from my kids."

Chapter Three

With last-minute preparations for the reunion guests, Christina had little time to dwell on Seth Austin's mercurial moods. Seemed he could go from caring and considerate to simmering animosity at the drop of a dusty Stetson.

Also, if she read the situation correctly, he still had unresolved feelings for his late wife. Or ex-wife. Or late ex-wife. Christina still wasn't totally clear on which label applied. And she definitely wasn't clear on why it should matter to her, because the last thing she needed in her life was a tall, good-looking cowboy with issues of his own.

Even if his two kids were adorably precious.

When the first of the weekend guests rolled in on Thursday afternoon, Christina thought it wise to get out of the way for a while. She snapped on Gracie's car harness and buckled her into the passenger seat, then headed for town.

Passing the spot where she'd first encountered Seth brought a quiver to her stomach, so she kept her eyes forward until she turned onto Main Street. Downtown Juniper Bluff appeared no busier now than it had been two days ago when she'd first driven through, which was a good thing because since the accident, Christina didn't easily abide noise and confusion—another reason she hoped moving to a small town would help her ease back into normal life.

The sun-dappled town square looked peacefully inviting. Christina parked on a side street and walked over with Gracie, and they followed the path to the foot of the horse-and-rider statue. Christina read the inscription on the plaque beneath.

Jake Austin.

Juniper Bluff's Hometown Hero.

According to the plaque, Austin was a search-and-rescue volunteer who met his death twenty-two years ago while freeing a family trapped in their overturned car.

A tremor raced through Christina as images from her own accident surfaced. Determinedly shaking them off, she focused on the man's features forever preserved in bronze. The resemblance to Seth was uncanny. Could Jake Austin be his father? If so, Seth would have been a young boy at the time, probably about Joseph's age. So very young to lose a parent.

Gracie nudged Christina's hand, the dog's quiet signal that she sensed Christina's tension level climbing. How an animal knew such things, Christina had no idea. She was grateful nonetheless and made a conscious effort to relax.

"Okay, girl, let's walk. After two days of maid's work, I need to stretch the kinks out."

After an hour or so of meandering around the square and peeking in a couple of interesting shops, they headed back to the car. Before leaving town, Christina stopped at the supermarket and picked up a rotisserie chicken and small container of three-bean salad. Marie had been cooking all day, and the family would have dinner in the main dining room with the ranch guests. Marie had invited Christina to join them, but Christina doubted she could endure the socializing—or Seth's annoyed glares—without her dog close by. A quiet supper in her cabin sounded much more appealing.

Hard work and tranquil surroundings were definitely conducive to a good night's sleep, and Christina awoke the next morning feeling more energized than she had in a long time. The sun had barely peeked over the hills when she trekked to the workroom to organize her housekeeping supplies. As soon as the guests had gone to the main house for breakfast, she trundled the maid's cart down the path and set to work. She easily finished making beds and freshening bathrooms in the two occupied cabins before the families returned.

Consulting her checklist, she made sure everything was in order in the other three cabins reserved for the weekend, then pushed the cart back to the workroom and deposited a pile of damp towels in the laundry bin. By then, her morning burst of energy had waned. Ready to put her feet up for a bit while sipping a cold drink, she trudged outside.

"Christina!" Marie called from the porch. "Can you come in the house for a minute and give me a hand with something?"

"Sure." Christina waved and started that way. The soft chair and cold drink would have to wait.

In the kitchen, Christina found Marie huddled over a red-faced, teary-eyed Joseph, perched on a chair at the end of the trestle table. The little boy cradled his left hand and refused to let Marie see it.

Christina hurried forward. "What happened?"

"He was playing in the barn and got a big ol' splinter. Now he won't let me pull it out."

"Ouch." Offering Joseph a sympathetic smile, Christina knelt in front of him, Gracie at her side. "If I promise not to touch it, would you hold your hand out for me to see?"

"Y-you promise?" He started to extend his hand, then jerked it back. "You can't let Omi touch it, either."

"Absolutely not. What if Omi and I both tuck our hands into our back pockets? Will you show us then?"

Joseph thought a moment, then nodded. He opened his left hand to reveal an ugly splinter embedded deep into his grime-covered palm. If they didn't get the splinter out and clean the wound, infection was sure to follow.

"Wow, that's pretty nasty," Christina murmured. She skewed her lips. "Hmm, seems to me you have two choices."

He looked up with a worried frown.

"Well, if you don't let Omi pull out the splinter and clean up your hand, you might have to go to the doctor for a shot."

Joseph gasped and tucked the injured hand beneath his other arm. "No shots!"

Marie patted the boy's shoulder. "Christina's right, I'm afraid. Please, Joseph—"

"But it'll hurt!"

"I have an idea," Christina said. "Whenever I'm scared or worried or hurting, I just hug on Gracie, and pretty soon I feel better. I bet she'd let you pet her while Omi takes care of your hand."

Swallowing, Joseph cast the dog a leery glance, then studied his palm. It seemed forever before he finally whispered, "Okay, I'll try."

With an inner sigh of gratitude, Christina rose and led Gracie around to Joseph's right side. "Now, then, you keep all your attention on Gracie and don't pay any mind to what Omi's doing."

She nodded at Marie, who stood ready with an alcohol-sterilized sewing needle and tweezers. Marie pulled a chair closer and sat down, then gently placed Joseph's injured hand on her lap. While Christina talked softly to the boy and had him stroke Gracie's soft fur, Marie quickly and efficiently plucked out the splinter.

Joseph looked around in surprise. "It's out?"

"Sure is!" Marie held up the wood fragment for him to see.

"It's…so big!" He grinned up at Christina. "And I didn't feel a thing."

She tousled his hair. "Thank Gracie. She's the best, isn't she?"

Marie stood. "Now we need to get you washed up and put some antibiotic ointment on your hand."

Joseph turned to Christina. "Can Gracie come, too?"

"Of course."

The three of them, plus Gracie, traipsed down the hall to the bathroom. After Marie finished treating the wound, they returned to the kitchen as Seth and Eva came in the back door.

At the sight of Gracie, Eva shrieked and leaped into Seth's arms. Shielding his little girl, Seth glowered at Christina.

This time she refused to be intimidated. "I'm sorry for scaring Eva, but my dog just saved your son from an infected wound."

Doubt clouding his eyes, Seth looked from Christina to his grandmother. "You got the splinter out?"

"We did." Marie patted Gracie's head. "Couldn't have done it without this sweet thing."

Now they had Eva's attention. Still clinging to her father's neck, she peeked down at Gracie, then shot her brother a worried frown.

"It's true, Eva," Joseph said. "I petted the dog the whole time Omi fixed my hand and it didn't hardly hurt at all!"

Marie reached for Eva. "Come on, sweetie, and I'll fix you kids some chocolate milk." Balancing the little girl on her hip, she raised a brow in Seth's direction. "Why don't you take Christina down to the picnic area and y'all can start setting up for tonight's barbecue."

Seth's expression said spending time with Christina was the last thing he cared to do, but he didn't argue. With a deferential nod, he extended one arm toward the back door. "After you."

Leave it to his grandmother to put him in yet another awkward position. Seth would have liked a little more time to accept the notion that Christina's dog had actually proved helpful. Although Joseph's surprisingly sunny attitude made it pretty clear.

In the barn earlier, when Seth first heard his son's yelp of pain, he'd tried to remove the splinter himself.

"No! Let Omi do it!" Joseph had screamed.

Seth had sent him on to the house, hoping his grandmother would get the deed done before Seth finished his barn chores and caught up. Times like these were when the kids most needed a mother's gentle touch. Omi was the next best thing, but Seth knew his son well enough to realize even Omi would have her hands full in this situation.

He cast a sidelong glance at the woman walking beside him. The words *thank you* sat on the tip of his tongue, but stubbornness prevented him from forcing them out.

Halfway to the lakeside picnic area, Christina broke the silence. "What exactly do we need to do out here?"

Halting in his tracks, Seth slapped a palm against his forehead and groaned. "It would help if I'd remembered to get the picnic supplies from the storeroom."

"I was wondering…" She offered a pert grin, and Seth figured he should be glad that was the worst of it.

"You can wait here if you want. Won't take me long."

"No, I'll help. I need to know where to find things."

"Suit yourself." Seth pivoted and strode toward the garage. He didn't look back to see if Christina followed, but the soft crunch of sneakers and dog paws on the gravel drive told him she wasn't far behind.

Rounding the garage, he stopped at the storeroom door and fumbled in his pockets.

"Something wrong?" Christina asked.

"Don't have my keys with me."

"Allow me." Nudging him aside, Christina used her set of housekeeping keys to unlock the door. She pushed it open, then mimicked his earlier gallantry to motion him inside.

"Thank you," he muttered.

She tilted her head, one brow arched accusingly. "There. That wasn't so hard, was it?"

With a roll of his eyes, Seth released a weak chuckle. "I deserved that. So let me try again. Thanks for getting the door. And thanks for helping get Joseph's splinter out."

"You're welcome. Now, where are those picnic supplies?"

A few minutes later, Seth had loaded three plastic crates and some cleaning supplies onto a utility wagon. Once again, they started for the lake, and this time the tension between them wasn't quite so thick. At the picnic area, the dog stretched out in the grass while Seth and Christina began wiping down tables and benches. Then Seth unfolded a blue gingham tablecloth. He took one end and handed Christina the other, and together they smoothed it across the first table. Seth found a container of specially made clips, which they used to secure the cloth in place.

The breeze shifted, and Christina paused to sniff the air. "Something smells wonderful!"

"That'd be the brisket Opi's smoking. Best in Texas, if you ask me."

"We have pretty good barbecue in Arkansas, too."

Seth scoffed as he shook out another tablecloth. "Only because of the Texans who moved there. And I bet y'all don't have sauce as good as what my grandmother makes."

Fastening down her side of the cloth, Christina winked. "Don't tell me—it's a secret family recipe."

"Wouldn't you like to know." Seth's hand brushed hers as he smoothed out a wrinkle, and he felt the tingle all the way to his knees. He quickly straightened, clearing his throat. "I should get back. I need to gather some wood for the fire pit."

"Oh. Okay." Did she sound a little bit disappointed? "Anything else I need to do here?"

"One of the crates has some table decorations. Candles and globes, flowers, greenery. You'll do better with those than I would."

Christina slanted him a teasing look of disdain. "Why? Because I'm a girl?"

"Believe me, you don't want to see the mess I'd make trying to put a centerpiece together."

"If you say so." Christina turned to peer inside one of the crates. She pulled out a handful of artificial bluebonnets and a box of candles. "What should I do with all this stuff when I finish?"

"I'll bring the wagon back with the firewood and then haul the crates to the storeroom." Hands on hips, he glanced around. "You'll probably be done before then, so just leave everything where it is."

As he turned to go, Christina called out to him. "Seth?"

"Yeah?"

"Thank you."

His forehead bunched. "For what?"

"For giving me a chance."

A fresh wave of guilt swept through him. "I haven't been real good about it so far, have I?"

"No, but I understand why now. And I'm in no position to judge."

Seth cringed as his grandmother's admonition came back to bite him. "I'm sure not, either." He paused while a beefy aroma drifted his way on the morning breeze. He had plenty of other things to do, but for some crazy reason he couldn't seem to get his feet moving. Pointing to the bluebonnet sprigs Christina was attempting to arrange around a candle globe, he said, "It works better if you use one of those Styrofoam thingies."

Christina looked up with an arched brow. "And you said you didn't know anything about centerpieces." Her expression softened into an endearing smile. "So will you give me a hand? Because I'm really not the artsy-craftsy type."

He opened his mouth to say yes, then snapped it shut. This was so not happening. Not again. Against his will, memories of Georgia crept in. He'd fallen for her during their junior year at Texas A&M, lured by crystal-blue eyes, silky blond hair and an invitation to help her stuff envelopes for a sorority fund-raiser she was heading up. Eight months later, they were married.

Eight *years* later, he'd found himself standing at his ex-wife's graveside and wondering how it had come to this. Wondering how he'd ever explain to his kids why they'd never see their mother again.

No, they'd had enough heartache in their short lives. Seth had experienced more than his share, too. He wouldn't risk letting another woman slip through the chinks in his armor.

"Whatever you do will be fine," he muttered.

Without a backward glance, he marched to the house. About time to check on his kids. Eva never liked him out of her sight for long and was probably pestering Omi about going to find her daddy right now.

He walked into the kitchen to a very different scene. While his grandmother stood at the counter chopping vegetables, Joseph and Eva perched on barstools and nibbled string cheese. Engrossed in her brother's recounting of his splinter experience and "Miss Christina's amazing doggy," Eva hardly acknowledged Seth's arrival.

The realization that he hadn't been missed—and the reason why—cut deep. For the space of a nanosecond, he forgot how to breathe.

"Hey, Seth." Omi's cheery greeting snapped him out of it. "How's it going with the picnic setup?"

"Fine. Christina's putting the centerpieces together."

"So what are you doing in here? Shouldn't you be helping?"

He swiped a carrot stick and bit off a piece, then chewed with a vengeance so he wouldn't have to answer right away. "She's managing," he mumbled over a mouthful, then grabbed a slice of zucchini.

Omi slapped his hand. "Those are for the barbecue tonight. And you shouldn't have left her on her own. She's still learning how we do things around here."

"Seems plenty capable to me." He wouldn't mention Christina's lopsided fake-bluebonnet arrangement.

The chopping knife came down hard on an unsuspecting green pepper. "Seth Jacob Austin, if you aren't the biggest scaredy-cat I ever did see."

He wouldn't deny it. Because he couldn't. So he didn't say anything, just spun on his heel and walked out.

Christina adjusted the greenery around a glass hurricane shade. She'd tried to tell Seth this wasn't her area of expertise, and now everyone at Serenity Hills Guest Ranch would realize it, too. With a groan of futility, she gathered up the leftover centerpiece materials and packed them into a crate.

Peering up the sloping path, she looked for signs of Seth's return. He'd stormed off so fast that he'd forgotten to take the utility wagon with him. Christina wondered when, or if, he'd return with his load of firewood and then help her get these crates back to the storeroom.

"Guess we're on our own, Gracie." Gripping the wagon handle, Christina dug deep for the strength to tow the unwieldy contraption up the hill.

By the time she reached the storeroom, her back and

shoulders ached and her left hip was cramping again. She moved one of the crates to the floor and sank onto it while she waited for the ache to subside.

Bryan Peterson appeared in the doorway, a concerned frown creasing his weathered face. "You okay, sweetheart?"

"Just taking a short break." Christina tried to smile as she massaged her hip. "Is there anything else you need me to do right now?" *Please say no.*

"We're in good shape. Marie might need a hand in the kitchen later, though. She's cookin' up a storm for the barbecue."

"I've been smelling the brisket all morning." Christina's stomach underscored her remark with a loud growl.

Bryan guffawed. "I'll take that as a compliment!" He ambled over to a shelf and poked around. "Say, that dog of yours sure made a hit with Joseph. Just came from the house, and he had to tell me all about how Gracie kept him from being scared while Omi doctored his hand."

Christina's chest warmed. She bent to give Gracie a hug around the neck and inhaled the comforting, musky-sweet scent of dog fur. "She's sure been a blessing to me."

Tugging a flat, oblong box from the shelf, Bryan asked, "How long have you had her?"

"Ever since I got out of rehab after the accident." Glancing away, Christina exhaled slowly as the memories resurfaced. "For a while, I was terrified to even ride in a car, much less drive again. But with Gracie beside me…somehow she keeps the fear at bay."

"Interesting. Sorry to say I didn't know much about service dogs for your kind of trauma before Marie explained how Gracie helps you." Lips skewed, Bryan looked toward the open door. "I worry about Seth's kids. Worry about him, too."

"That's understandable." Christina hesitated. "I guess you know in my former life I was a social worker. My specialty was children and families."

"Yeah, Marie mentioned it was on your job application." A nervous look flickered behind his eyes. "Best you don't bring it up around Seth, though. He's not too keen on social workers."

"Really? Why?" Christina couldn't fathom why any parent with kids as emotionally wounded as Seth's would refuse whatever help he could find.

"Long story," Bryan said with a sigh, "and I probably shouldn't be telling it, but since Seth won't talk about it, seems somebody ought to."

He set down his box, pulled over a step stool and plopped down. Speaking in hushed tones, and with repeated glances toward the door, he described how Georgia Austin's career had taken off and she'd urged Seth to move the family to Minneapolis. He'd refused, insisting their home was here in Juniper Bluff, and if she truly loved him and the kids, she wouldn't need a fancy job in a big city to feel complete.

"Seth fought long and hard to save his marriage," Bryan went on. "Fought even harder for custody of those kids. Then Georgia got sick, and that's when a social worker stepped in. She convinced Georgia the kids would be better off with Georgia's sister and her husband, who had a nice home in Tulsa and boy-and-girl twins a couple years older than Joseph."

"A ready-made family," Christina acknowledged with a nod.

"Exactly. A far sight better, in her opinion, than placing the kids with an angry, broken single dad and his aging grandparents on a barely-making-it guest ranch."

"Obviously, Seth won."

Bryan's mouth hardened. "Almost didn't. Between the social worker and the high-powered lawyers Georgia's family hired, he had the fight of his life." Groaning, he pushed to his feet and hefted the box he'd come for. With a kindly but pointed glance at Christina, he stated, "So, like I said, best not mention the social worker thing around Seth."

Left alone in the storeroom, she massaged her hip while pondering everything she'd learned about this troubled family in the three short days since her arrival. Her initial thoughts about God's having brought her here for a reason now gave way to doubt, because she suspected Seth would never be open to the kind of help she'd been trained to give.

For all the good her training had done her personally. The adage *physician, heal thyself* played through her mind. A master's degree and four years' on-the-job experience hadn't prepared her for the aftermath of the accident that nearly cost her life—and not only hers but that of the innocent child in her care.

A stabbing pain arced through her skull. Even with both fists pressed to her temples, she couldn't halt the parade of images behind her eyelids, or the voices screaming in her head.

"I'm taking Haley to the hospital, Mr. Vernon. Please don't try to stop me. The police are on their way."

"She's my kid! You got no right to lay a hand on her!"

But the brute of a man already had, and more than once, judging from the blood and bruises. As Christina carried the sobbing child toward the car, the ominous click of a shotgun hurried her steps. She'd barely gotten Haley buckled into a child safety seat when the first blast from the gun rang in her ears.

Before the second shot, she was behind the wheel, gunning the engine and barreling down the potholed lane.

She never even saw the loaded dump truck bearing down on them, only heard the scream of the horn, her own terrified shriek, and the crunch of collapsing metal and shattering glass before everything went black.

At Gracie's whimpers and insistent nudges, Christina wrapped her trembling arms around the dog's neck. Without the strength to stand, much less get herself to her cabin, she could do nothing more than hold on and wait—*pray!*—for the memories to pass. As she had every moment of her life since that day, she thanked God that little Haley Vernon had suffered only a broken arm as a result of the crash. The child now resided with a loving aunt and uncle in South Carolina, safely beyond her abusive father's reach.

From somewhere far away, a man's voice penetrated. "Christina, can you hear me? Are you okay?"

She lifted her head and met Seth's worried gaze. Ignoring the high-pitched hum in her ears, she dredged deep for what little control she could muster. "I'm…fine. A dizzy spell, that's all. I—I think I'm dehydrated."

Before she could blink twice, a bottle of water appeared in Seth's hand—where it came from, she had no idea. Kneeling in front of her, he unscrewed the top and helped her tip the bottle to her lips. "Better? Honestly, you don't look so good."

The kind and gentle Seth was back, but much as she appreciated this side of him, right now she'd have preferred a little more gruffness. If he were any nicer to her, she'd melt into a soggy puddle of tears. With great care, she forced herself to stand. "Really, I'm okay. I just need to lie down for a while."

"And eat something. It's past noon." He tucked a steadying hand at her elbow, which was a good thing because her legs felt like overcooked noodles. "I'm sorry I left you by yourself earlier. Let me walk you to your cabin."

If she refused, he might end up scraping her off the path and towing her to the cabin in his utility wagon. To keep her dignity intact, she muttered a terse "Okay, thanks," and hoped he didn't notice how heavily she leaned on him. "Let's go, Gracie."

Chapter Four

For Seth, the reunion weekend went by in a blur. What with serving barbecue, leading trail rides, and acting as lifeguard for lake swimmers and kayakers—plus making sure to give his kids plenty of attention—he had little time to dwell on what had happened with Christina. He tried to be polite whenever they crossed paths in the course of their ranch duties, but after her meltdown on Friday, she seemed even more uncomfortable around him than before.

Seth had to admire the woman's work ethic, though. She'd toiled as hard as any of them, keeping the guest cabins in top-notch order and helping Omi with meal preparation and anything else that needed doing. Christina had proved herself a reliable employee and a master of efficiency, and since this was admittedly her first job as a maid, Seth couldn't help wondering what she'd done previously. Since Omi wasn't forthcoming, maybe one of these days he'd sneak a peek at Christina's personnel file.

The last of the reunion attendees left late Sunday afternoon, and by Tuesday morning the post-weekend cleanup was complete and Serenity Hills lay in restful silence befitting its name. While his kids slept, Seth carried his first cup of coffee out to the porch swing, where he could savor a melon-colored dawn as the sun crept over the barn roof. This was his favorite time of day, a few precious moments to himself before tackling the never-ending ranch work. He loved it, though. Loved the clean air with a hint of cedar on the breeze, loved spending time with the horses, loved watching the stress of city life slowly slip from the ranch guests' shoulders as they basked in country hospitality.

Most of all, he loved sharing all this with his kids.

He would have shriveled up and died in Minneapolis. Or at least he'd have wanted to. And the certainty of it made his stomach clench. For the sake of his marriage, though—for the sake of his kids—he should have tried. *Lord, I'm sorry. I should have tried.*

He doubted he'd ever forgive himself for his own stubbornness.

Worse, he still struggled to forgive Georgia for leaving and then dying before he had the chance to fix things between them.

The regrets stuck in his throat, and not even scalding-hot coffee could budge them. This was the downside of quiet moments, when the past intruded and all the what-ifs started playing through his mind. Best get to work and cast the memories aside.

By the time Seth made it to the barn, Rafael, one of the ranch's part-time stable hands, had already taken several horses out to their pastures and had started mucking stalls. Seth snapped halters and lead ropes on two mares, then halted outside the stall where Rafael worked. "Leave Tango in for now. I'll ride her in a bit."

Rafael nodded as he scooped up soiled shavings with

a pitchfork. "You want me to groom her for you when I finish here?"

"That's okay. I'll enjoy doing it myself." Seth had been raised to believe a cowboy should tend to his own mount. Besides, applying brush and currycomb to horse hide had a certain calming effect on his psyche.

Leaving the barn, he led the mares down the lane to the pasture nearest Christina's cabin. Her windows remained dark, which shouldn't raise any red flags since Omi had given her the day off. Still, as hard as Christina had worked the past few days, Seth hoped she was only sleeping in and hadn't suffered some sort of stress-related setback. He hadn't forgotten how pale and shaky she'd been when he found her in the storeroom last week.

Then a window lit up, and moments later Christina stepped out to the porch, the dog at her side. Noticing Seth, she offered a tentative smile. He acknowledged her with a nod as he latched the pasture gate. While he hung the halters he'd just removed over the fence rail, Christina and her dog ambled toward him.

"Beautiful morning," she called as she drew near. "But I'm sorry I slept through the sunrise. That's been one of my favorite parts of working here so far."

"Not typically an early riser?" Seth took an inordinate amount of time looping the dangling lead ropes just so. Better that than getting distracted by sunlight on honey-gold hair. And he wasn't referring to Gracie the golden retriever.

Christina's soft sigh mingled with the morning breeze. "I've been a little too pampered the last couple of years. Anyway, suburban sunrises aren't quite the same."

"Guess not." Tipping his hat, Seth stepped past her. "Best get to it. Enjoy your day off."

"Thanks, I was thinking I'd—"

He didn't hang around to hear the rest. Double-timing it back to the barn, he reasoned he'd performed due diligence by assuring himself of Christina's well-being. Now he could put her out of his mind.

Except he couldn't. Now that things had settled down after the busy weekend, Seth found his thoughts drifting to the pretty new housekeeper a lot more often than he felt comfortable with. He'd like to chalk up his interest to idle curiosity—friendly concern at most. But his gut was telling him something different. Since Georgia, he'd pretty much closed off his heart where women were concerned. Not that relationship prospects were all that plentiful in a small town like Juniper Bluff, although there were two or three single gals he'd attended high school with who were quick to turn up the charm whenever he came around. They were nice enough women, if a little too marriage-minded, but he saw no kindness in giving them false hope.

He'd gotten an earful from Omi more than once about how it was high time he took himself off the shelf, if not for himself, then at least so his kids could know a mother's love again. If he ever did decide to take another chance on marriage—which he definitely did not see happening anytime soon—the only good reason would be for his kids' sake. Omi and Opi weren't getting any younger, and Seth depended greatly on their help with parenting. When they weren't around anymore…

Well, it didn't bear thinking about.

With Tango saddled up, Seth nudged the blue roan quarter horse into a trot and headed to the practice arena. He'd been training the mare for the Western Pleasure competition and had high hopes of placing in the next show. He planned to start breeding Tango next year, and successful showings would nudge up the value of her foals. Every dollar they brought would make it that much easier to keep the guest ranch in the black.

"Her top line's improving." Opi stood with his bad leg propped on a fence rail. Joseph and Eva had climbed up beside him and watched with big grins as Seth put Tango through her paces.

He circled closer to the rail. "She's coming along. Still a little poppy in the rear, but not like she was when we first started training."

"Daddy," Joseph called, "will you take us riding today?"

"Maybe. Let me finish with Tango first." Adjusting pressure on the right rein, Seth coaxed the horse to straighten her shoulder, then transitioned from the jog into a long trot and began a figure-eight pattern across the arena.

When he came around again, he glimpsed Christina and her dog striding over. When Eva saw the dog, she screeched and clambered higher up the fence. The commotion caused Tango to shy and skitter sideways. A less experienced rider would have hit the dirt.

"Easy, girl. Easy!" Seth used seat and reins to get the horse under control.

Tightening her hold on the leash, Christina guided the dog several feet away. "I'm so sorry," she called. "I just wanted to watch, and I—I forgot about Eva."

"Well, you *can't* forget." Jaw clenched, Seth dismounted and marched to the rail. He lifted Eva into his arms, putting a six-foot rail fence between his trembling daughter and the dog.

Opi's frown spoke his disappointment. "Christina

didn't mean any harm, Seth. Eva was just startled, that's all. No need to overreact."

Overreact? Since when was protecting his kids over-reacting? While he bit his tongue to keep from snapping at his grandfather, Joseph jumped down from the fence and trotted over to Christina.

Dropping to his knees, the boy hugged the big yellow dog around the neck. Over his shoulder, he yelled, "Look, Eva. Gracie's being really sweet. She's not mean at all. Remember how she helped me with my splinter?"

Next thing Seth knew, Eva was wriggling out of his arms. She tiptoed to the rail. "If you bring her right here to the fence, would she let me touch her?"

"Sure she would." Joseph tugged on Christina's hand. "Bring Gracie over so Eva can pet her."

"I don't know, Joseph…" Worry lines creased the corners of Christina's mouth. She met Seth's stare with an uneasy frown.

Didn't seem to matter what Seth thought. Eva now stood within arm's reach of the fence. As she shyly stretched her hand between the rails, Joseph guided it to Gracie's head. "See how soft she is? Just pet her, Eva. She's a good dog."

Seth prepared to swoop in and rescue his little girl at the first sign of trouble. Only there wasn't any. He held his breath as Eva inched closer, using both hands to caress the dog's floppy ears.

"She's so soft," Eva cooed. Then she giggled. "Look, Daddy, I think she's smiling at me."

"Yeah, it kinda looks like it." Seth braved a glance at Christina, and the look she returned about did him in. Part apology, part I-told-you-so, part pure joy.

Oblivious to her father's internal struggle, Eva motioned him over. "Come pet her, Daddy. I bet she'll like you, too."

Jaw clenched, he joined his daughter at the fence. One hand on Eva's shoulder and dropping to one knee, he slid his other hand onto Gracie's head. The dog whipped out a wet, pink tongue and swiped it across his wrist. Eva laughed louder, and when she held out her own fingers for the dog to lick, Seth couldn't have been more stunned if his little girl had sprouted wings.

"Eva," Joseph prodded, "come on this side so you can pet her better."

Instantly, Eva drew back, shrinking into the shelter of Seth's arms. "No, I'd be too scared!"

Christina lowered herself to eye level with Eva. "It's okay, sweetie. Gracie doesn't mind at all if you'd rather pet her through the fence. Or maybe sometimes I can bring her over to your backyard and you can pet her with the porch rails between you. How does that sound?"

Eva looked to Seth for reassurance before giving a tentative nod.

Then a snort sounded behind him, and horse slime slithered down his shirt collar. While he squeezed his eyes shut with a disgusted groan, laughter surrounded him. "Yeah, yeah, very funny." Pushing up from the ground, he grabbed the reins dangling from his neglected horse's bridle. "Sorry, Tango. Haven't forgotten you, girl."

"Can we go riding now, Dad?" Joseph pleaded. "And can Christina and Gracie go with us?"

Christina took a step back, and any remaining shred of confidence disappeared. "Oh, I don't think—"

"You're a ranch girl now," Opi insisted with a grin. "Gonna have to give it a try sooner or later. And you couldn't have a better teacher than Seth."

* * *

Not sure how it happened, and definitely wondering why she'd gone along with the idea, Christina found herself on horseback. Sugarbear, she'd been informed, was a sorrel gelding and the gentlest horse on the place.

"Nothing to worry about," Seth's grandfather insisted as he adjusted her stirrups. "You can hold right there to the saddle horn. Long as you sit tall and don't drop the reins, Sugarbear will follow right along with the other horses."

"Sit tall. Don't drop the reins," Christina repeated. The hard-shell safety helmet Bryan had buckled under her chin only served to remind her that horseback riding could be dangerous. Didn't matter that on Saturday she'd watched an eighty-five-year-old grandmother eagerly climb into the saddle to ride this very same horse and live to brag about it.

Seth's kids certainly showed no fear, at least not of horses and riding, which was one huge reason Christina felt she had to go through with this. How could she hope to help these children overcome their deepest fears if she refused to face her own?

Joseph grinned at her from atop Spot, an aptly named Appaloosa pony that strongly resembled an overgrown Dalmatian. Seth held Eva in front of him on Tango. Both children wore helmets like Christina's, which stirred grudging appreciation for Seth's protective parenting—this aspect, at least.

"Y'all ready to ride?" Seth shot a glance her way, the same look she'd seen last weekend as he sized up the ranch guests' horsemanship skills. Or lack thereof, as in Christina's case.

"We're not going far, are we?" She released her grip

on the saddle horn long enough to make sure her helmet sat securely.

"A couple miles or so. Same trail we use for all the greenhorns." Was that a snicker she heard beneath his words?

Bryan patted the toe of Christina's sneaker before stepping out of the way. "You'll be fine. Enjoy the scenery."

The trail led past the lakeside picnic area and across a shallow creek, then zigzagged upward along an easy hillside slope. Cedars, live oaks and junipers fought for toeholds in the rocky soil. A squirrel chattered overhead, catching Gracie's attention as she trotted along beside Sugarbear, but the dog did no more than look up and sniff the air. She must have understood Christina still needed her on alert.

From somewhere in the distance came the *tap-tap-tap* of a woodpecker.

"Do you think it's a pileated?" Joseph asked.

Seth cocked his ear toward the sound. "Probably a ladder-backed. Never seen a pileated woodpecker around here."

"Rats. I really want to see one in real life."

"I've seen one," Christina said. The casual conversation had helped her relax a little. "There's a nature preserve near where I live in Arkansas, and you can spot them in the tops of the pine trees."

"Cool! Dad, can we go there sometime?"

Following behind Seth, Christina thought she detected the slightest tensing across his shoulders. "No need to go all the way to Arkansas," he said stiffly. "There are plenty of pine trees and pileated woodpeckers in Texas."

"Well, then, can we—"

"Let's talk about it later, son." Seth's tone was gentle but left no room for argument.

His negativity grated on Christina. Even with what Bryan had told her about Seth's bitter custody battle, this apparent compulsion to shield his children from new experiences wasn't healthy. Not for the children, and not for Seth.

Maybe it would be wise to change the subject. They'd crested the hill and now rode abreast through a broad meadow of coarse brown grasses. "Doesn't look like you've had much rain this summer," Christina remarked.

"Some years are drier than others." Seth kept his eyes forward and continued across the field.

Five more minutes of silence and Christina decided to try another tack. "So, Joseph, school must be starting in a couple of weeks. Will you be in third grade or fourth?"

"Fourth, but I don't go to the real school. Daddy and Omi teach me."

"Oh." Homeschooling certainly had its merits, but Christina had a feeling Seth had chosen this option for all the wrong reasons.

She'd about decided there was no safe conversation topic where Seth Austin was concerned, when he halted his horse abruptly and turned to her with a challenging grin. "Tell us more about yourself, Christina. What did you do before you came to work at Serenity Hills?"

"I was recovering from my accident," she answered carefully. At Gracie's whimper, she took a slow, deep breath before continuing. "These last two years have meant a lot of hard work and more than a few adjustments. That's why I'm especially grateful to your grandmother for giving me this job and a chance to put my life back together."

Seth's jaw muscles flexed. He glanced down, then up

again, and his expression softened. "I sometimes forget others have been through hard times, too."

Eva had been quiet for most of the ride but now reached up to pat Seth's cheek. "It's okay, Daddy. If you get sad, you should just pet Gracie and she'll make it all better."

A strangled laugh burst from Christina's throat, while at the same time her eyes welled with unexpected tears.

Seth covered his daughter's hand with his own and winked at Christina, surprising her with a smile. "Out of the mouths of babes, huh?"

"You'd be amazed how much wiser children are about some things than we are."

With a thoughtful nod, Seth wheeled Tango around and continued across the meadow. Sugarbear, the ideal trail horse, followed without any prompting from Christina, and she had to admit she'd felt perfectly safe on the horse's back.

At least until Seth grinned over his shoulder and suggested, "Ready to go a little faster?"

"No!" Christina locked her fingers around the saddle horn.

"Aw, come on," Joseph urged. "Fast is more fun!" He tapped his pony's sides, and Spot took off at a bouncy trot.

Sugarbear's muscles quivered with his eagerness to keep up, and Christina fought a wave of panic. Gracie had already picked up on her agitation and instinctively tried to block the horse's forward movement. Now concerned for her dog's safety, Christina called, "Please, can't we just keep it at a walk?"

Seth shouted at Joseph to slow down, then turned and

rode back to Christina. With a restraining hand on Sugar-bear's reins, he spoke quietly to the horse until he settled.

"I—I'm sorry," Christina gasped, her heart thudding. All she wanted was to get down off this horse and bury her face in Gracie's neck.

"Hang on, it's all right." In one swift movement Seth swung himself and Eva to the ground. After planting Eva firmly out of the way of the horses, he came up beside Sugarbear and held up his hands to Christina. "Let's take a break. I'll help you down."

Too relieved to think beyond the moment, she transferred her grip from the saddle horn to Seth's broad shoulders. With his strong arms supporting her, she slid from the saddle and collapsed against him.

"Easy, easy." Seth soothed her with gentle pats as if she were a jittery colt. "Man, you're really shaking. Never meant to scare you like that."

Aware of Gracie's wet nose on her elbow, Christina freed one arm from Seth's protective hold and clutched the dog's ruff. As her breathing slowed, she became all too aware of Seth's firm chest beneath her cheek, along with the steady, reassuring beat of his heart. If she thought her legs would hold her, she ought to put some distance between them. He was her employer, after all. Besides, how many times would he come to her rescue like this before he convinced his grandmother she was unfit for the job?

Feeling steadier, she gripped his biceps—another mistake, considering how her pulse spiked—and pushed away. Unable to meet his gaze, she mumbled an apology. "We should probably head back now…somehow."

Somehow, of course, meant climbing into the saddle again, and Christina would almost rather walk the whole way.

Joseph rode up behind his father. "Dad, is Miss Christina okay?"

"She'll be fine, son." Still bracing Christina by her forearms, Seth peered hard at her as if to convince himself. "We've got to remember she doesn't ride every day like we do."

Christina straightened and cleared her throat. "I've been on a horse before." She struck a defensive pose. "Once. When I was...nine."

Seth's lips twitched. As he shared a look with Joseph, a rumble began in his throat, and they both laughed out loud. Turning to lift Eva into his arms, Seth said, "These kids have been riding since they were nine *months* old. When Eva turns seven in a few months, she's getting her own pony."

"I want a yellow one with a pink mane," Eva stated. "Like this one." She pulled a tiny toy pony from her pocket and held it out to Christina.

"Oh, that's adorable." Feeling more herself, Christina shared a teasing look with Seth as she gave the toy pony's nose an admiring pat. "When your daddy finds a real pony with a pink mane like this, I'll be first in line to see it."

"Don't hold your breath." Seth's smile softened, and he cocked a brow. "Think you can handle Sugarbear at a slow walk back to the barn?"

Christina sucked in a breath. "Key words being *slow* and *walk*."

"You got it."

Once Seth had delivered Christina safely back to the barn, she and her dog slipped away before he could make sure the horseback ride hadn't totally traumatized her. She'd seemed all right, even joined in the conversation as Seth pointed out interesting wildlife along the trail. He'd found himself speaking in the same easygoing tone he used to distract Eva whenever she got scared.

It felt entirely different to focus his concern on an adult woman, though—an attractively intriguing woman who did unnerving things to his insides. He could still feel her trembling against him in those moments after he'd helped her down from the horse. If not for his experience with Eva's fear and shyness, he'd have a much harder time empathizing with what Christina must be going through.

But did he want to? It would sure be easier if he didn't find himself caring so much. How could he not like and admire her for the inner strength she exhibited—yes, even in the face of his surliness about her dog?

As Opi helped Seth and Joseph put away tack and brush down the horses, Omi came out to ask how the ride went. Seth answered with a noncommittal "Fine," and when Omi gave up prodding him for more, she took the children to the house to start lunch.

Opi proved a little harder to evade. "Christina sure took off in a hurry. Hope you didn't insult her again."

"I did *not* insult her." Seth grabbed a broom to sweep some loose straw out of the barn aisle. "I think she actually enjoyed herself…mostly."

"Mostly?" Opi snorted. "What exactly did happen out there on the trail? It's just you and me now, so spit it out."

"It was nothing, all right? She got a little shook up when Joseph wanted to go faster. We had a—a moment." Seth's fists tightened around the broom handle as he remembered holding Christina in his arms.

Cornering Seth between a tack trunk and a stall gate, Opi fixed him with a cool stare. "You're starting to like Christina, aren't you?"

"What's not to like? She's turning out to be a real good housekeeper." Seth plied the broom around his grandfather's boots. "You're in my way."

"You're getting in your own way, if you ask me." Opi rolled his eyes and stepped aside.

"I suppose that's a commentary on my personal life?"

"Hmm, that would imply you actually had a personal life."

Seth glared at his grandfather. "Now who's getting insulting?"

"Just sayin'." Whistling the tune to a romantic country ballad Seth had been hearing on the radio, Opi sauntered out of the barn.

"Old coot." Seth aimed a swift kick to the barn wall.

When the toe of his boot splintered a rotting board, his frustration was instantly redirected. Just one more sign of all that needed to be done to keep this place up and running. With business declining over the past couple of years, the ranch had done well to cover basic operating costs. Add unanticipated repairs on top of routine maintenance, and expenses shot up faster than a rodeo cowboy getting thrown from an angry bull.

Personal life? No time for anything beyond being the best dad he could be while making sure the ranch would still be here for his kids someday.

Chapter Five

With three of the cabins reserved for the following weekend, by midweek activity around the ranch had picked up again. Seth spent a good portion of his time making repairs in and around the barn, which allowed for some quality father/son time with Joseph. The kid was getting pretty good at slinging a hammer, and when Seth enlisted his help measuring boards, it offered a chance to work on Joseph's math skills. They hadn't slacked off completely on schoolwork over the summer, but it would soon be time to return to a more consistent homeschooling routine.

The thought reminded him of the subtle tightening of Christina's lips when the subject of school came up during their horseback ride. Was she not in favor of homeschooling in general, or was this another judgment on Seth's overprotective parenting?

He couldn't let it bother him. Didn't he have the right to raise his kids as he thought best?

On Thursday morning as Seth headed to the toolshed to find another two-by-four for his barn repairs, he glanced toward the house and saw Christina sitting on the bottom porch step, Gracie stretched out at her feet. He didn't think anything of it until the back door opened and Omi came out with Eva.

Seth tensed for Eva's scream and quick retreat into the safety of the house.

It didn't happen.

Releasing Omi's hand, Eva crept down the steps and settled next to Christina. Seth held his breath while his smiling little girl put her arms around the dog's neck and accepted wet doggy kisses.

Okay, so this shouldn't have come as a complete surprise. For the past few days Eva had grown more and more comfortable petting the dog through the porch rail, just as Christina had suggested. But to see his child so perfectly at ease, nothing separating her from the animal who only days ago had sent her leaping into the arms of the nearest adult—well, it was nothing short of amazing.

Joseph called to him from the barn door. "You coming, Dad?"

Still awestruck, he nodded toward the house. "See that?"

"Yeah, cool." The boy didn't sound nearly as impressed as Seth. "Eva likes Gracie now. Miss Christina's been taking them on walks sometimes."

How had Seth missed that? "Really? When?"

Joseph's mouth quirked. "Um, once while you were training Tango, I think. And yesterday when you took me with you to the hardware store. Eva told me after we got back."

Guess it proved how preoccupied Seth had been with ranch chores. Or maybe he wasn't as attentive a father as he liked to believe.

"Da-ad." Joseph made a growling noise. "You said you were getting a board."

Obviously, his son was *getting bored* waiting on Seth to

get his head back in the game. "What do you say we take a break? We can get a cold drink and say hi to Chri—to Eva."

"Great!" Joseph took off at a jog, and Seth was glad the boy hadn't tuned in on his slip of the tongue.

Yep, that's all it was, a slip of the tongue, and nobody—including himself—had better read anything more into it.

By the time Seth caught up, Joseph had dropped to his knees next to Gracie and was rubbing his face against her fur. He and Eva both giggled as the dog literally lapped up their affection.

Christina looked up with an uncertain smile. "Hi."

"Hi yourself." Hands on hips, Seth shot a meaningful glance at his grandmother, seated on the top step. "I feel like I missed a huge milestone in my daughter's life."

"You've been busy," Omi replied.

Her tone put Seth on the defensive. "Things needed doing."

Christina stood. "I think that's my cue to get back to work. Kids, Gracie and I—"

"Hang on." Seth pressed his eyes closed briefly as annoyance gave way to gratitude. "Sorry, guess I'm still in shock. I haven't seen Eva hugging on a dog this way since before—" His breath caught. "Anyway, thank you."

"You're welcome." Christina's chin shifted. "You know, I—never mind."

"No, say it." Letting his shoulders fall, Seth forced himself to meet her gaze. "After what I just witnessed here, you have a perfect right to tell me exactly what you think."

She flicked a glance toward the children, then lowered her voice. "It can wait."

Omi pushed up from the step. "Who wants to help me bake some oatmeal-raisin cookies?"

"Me! Me!" the kids yelled as they darted up the steps.

As Omi herded the children inside, she glanced back at Seth. "I'm getting low on flour and eggs. Can you run into town and pick some up?"

"Now? I'm not finished in the barn."

"Yes, *now*," Omi answered with a mischievous smile. "And take Christina with you. I'm sure she could use a few things from the market, too."

This was a setup, pure and simple. Seth braved a glance at Christina. "If you've got other things to do…"

"She doesn't," Omi snapped. "Now both of you, get going." The door slammed behind her.

Christina's heartless chuckle broke the sudden silence. "Your grandmother is a force of nature."

"That she is." With a pained sigh, Seth started up the porch steps. "Gotta get my wallet and keys. Meet you at my truck in five minutes?"

"Can we make it ten? I need to freshen up and grab my purse. Oh, and you do know I'll be bringing Gracie, right?"

Seth turned with a slow smile. "Sure, ten minutes is fine. And no worries. After hauling around two messy kids and a passel of smelly horse gear, I'm not about to sweat a little dog hair."

"Then I guess it's a d—" Christina clamped her lips together. "I mean, see you in ten."

Watching Christina start down the lane, Seth paused a moment while the dreaded D-word—*date*—rumbled around in his brain. If Omi thought she could blast him out of bachelorhood so easily, she had another think coming.

Standing before the dresser mirror, Christina yanked out her ponytail holder and snatched up her hairbrush. She couldn't believe she almost said the word *date* out loud—and to Seth! Even if either of them could possibly be interested, Christina had been a career woman long enough to know you didn't date your employer. The implications were simply too problematic.

Gracie pranced over and dropped her fuzzy ball at Christina's feet, then looked up with mischief in her eyes. Or something else, as if the dog knew something Christina didn't.

"Don't get any ideas, girl." Christina picked up the squishy, slobbery dog toy and rolled it across the floor for Gracie to chase. She loved the playful side of her service dog. Gracie always seemed to know when to be on alert and when she could just be a dog.

And sometimes, like now, Gracie's playfulness turned out to be exactly what Christina needed to stay grounded.

Leaving her hair loose about her shoulders, she applied a quick swipe of lip gloss, then grabbed her purse. Gracie followed her out the door, and they stopped at the car for Gracie's seat belt harness.

Seth met them at his pickup and opened the door behind the passenger seat. "Will she be okay in back?"

"That's fine." Christina knelt to slip Gracie into her harness. Sensing Seth watching, she looked up with a smirk. "Yes, she wears a seat belt. I'm an overprotective parent, too."

Seth harrumphed. "I didn't say a word."

A few minutes later, they were on the road to Juniper Bluff. Christina hadn't exactly expected scintillating conversation from Seth, but she was hoping for more than stolen glances at his stoic profile while they drove in silence. Noticing a cache of CDs in the center console, she picked one up. "You're a country music fan?"

He peered briefly at the CD case then returned his attention to the road. "Guess you could say so."

Really? That was all she was getting out of him? She pursed her lips and tried again. "Afraid I don't know much about country music. Almost everything on my playlist is Christian pop."

"Mmm."

Exhaling softly, Christina gazed out the side window. This was going nowhere faster than the fence posts zipping by.

Eons later, it seemed, Seth turned onto Main Street. "Need anything besides groceries while we're in town?"

The sudden sound of his voice jolted her. "Can't think of anything."

The town square now lay on their left, and as they passed the horse-and-rider statue, Christina thought she glimpsed a subtle tightening of Seth's jaw.

"I've been wanting to ask," she began softly, "is Jake Austin a relative of yours?"

Seth cleared his throat as he looked toward the statue. "My dad."

"I read the plaque the other day. He must have been quite a man."

"He was." The truck slowed. "Mind if we stop here for a minute? I haven't paid my respects lately."

"Not at all."

Seth parked across the street from the square, then came around to help Christina and Gracie to the pavement. Together they walked over and followed the path to the statue. Hat in hand, Seth stood gazing up at the image of his father for so long that Christina wondered if he'd forgotten she was there.

Then he sighed deeply and turned to her, his expression much more serene. "Thanks," he said. "Spending time with Dad always helps me put things in perspective."

"I'm sorry you had to grow up without him."

"Yeah, it was tough." Seth started walking but didn't appear in a hurry to get back to the pickup. "I'm about two shots of caffeine short for the day. Feel like some coffee before we head over to the market?"

"Okay." Surprised he was voluntarily extending their time in town together, Christina hurried to catch up.

When they'd crossed to the other side of the square, Seth followed the sidewalk to Diana's Donuts, and the aromas emanating from the shop reminded Christina that breakfast had been hours ago.

As they stepped inside, a couple of customers cast uneasy looks at Gracie. "It's all right," Seth stated. "She's a service dog."

Christina slanted him a curious look. Seth Austin was just full of surprises today.

"Seth Austin, as I live and breathe," called a perky brunette from behind the counter. "You haven't stopped in for ages. Where've you been keeping yourself?"

"Summertime, you know. We stay busy at the ranch." The confidence he'd exuded moments before seemed to wither under the woman's flirtatious grin.

"So business is good?" The brunette slid a quick glance toward Christina, a question in her eyes.

"We're doing all right. Can we get a couple of coffees, please?" He turned to Christina. "Want a doughnut or anything?"

She'd been too distracted by the interplay between Seth and his admirer to check out the selections. The glass case to the left of the cash register held an array of glazed and filled doughnuts, apple fritters, éclairs, muffins and Danish pastries. "It all looks good. What do you recommend?"

"Seth usually has a carrot muffin." The woman looked Christina up and down. "You look like a cheese Danish girl to me. And I think it's high time Seth introduced us."

He coughed into his fist. "Excuse me. Diana Matthews, meet Christina Hunter. Christina's the new housekeeper out at the ranch."

"Nice to meet you, Diana." Christina ignored the arched brow Diana shot in Gracie's direction. "And a cheese Danish sounds great."

Diana slid open the door on her side of the bakery case. "Pleased to meet you, too, and welcome to Juniper Bluff. First pastry and coffee is always on the house for our newcomers." She handed Christina a Danish on a paper plate, then reached for one of the carrot muffins.

"Not today, Diana," Seth interrupted. "Just coffee, thanks."

Looking disappointed, Diana carried two tall mugs to the coffee machine. When she returned, Seth handed her a couple of bills and told her to keep the change, then motioned Christina to an empty table near the front window.

"Diana seems nice." Christina swallowed a bite of her Danish. "Have you known her long?"

"We went to high school together. She was homecoming queen my senior year on the football team."

With a sidelong glance toward the woman behind the counter, Christina nodded. "Homecoming queen. Yes, I can believe it." Then she narrowed her eyes at Seth. "However, I can't quite picture you playing football."

Seth squared his shoulders. "Why not? Don't I look tough enough?"

"Oh, you look plenty tough." Heat rose in Christina's

cheeks. She'd like to blame the hot coffee but knew differently. "I just meant…um…" Now was not the time to make disparaging remarks about jocks. "I mean, you're so involved with horses and ranching."

"Guess you wouldn't know that some of the top pro football players started out as farm kids."

"Actually, I wouldn't know much about football at all." She cast him a sheepish glance. "So you were good?"

"Not particularly. Always a second-stringer." A chuckle rumbled in Seth's throat. "I was too involved with horses and ranching."

As they shared a smile, Diana sauntered over with a coffeepot. "Refills, anyone?"

Christina declined, but Seth held out his mug. "Thanks, Di."

"My pleasure. How are those kiddos doing?"

"Fine. Growing like weeds."

"You should bring them by sometime." Diana shot a concerned look toward Gracie, lying beside Christina's chair. "Wow. Poor little Eva. She must be scared to death having a big dog on the place. How are you managing?"

Seth winked at Christina. "You'd be surprised. I think Eva's got a new best friend."

Ignoring Diana's confused stare, Christina chose instead to bask in Seth's newfound approval. She liked this more agreeable side of him. Maybe, in time, they might even become friends.

Seth really wished Diana would go bake some more doughnuts or something. Instead, she seemed intent on hovering with her coffeepot and making small talk.

He also didn't appreciate the way she kept eyeing

Christina and the dog like she had to protect Seth and his kids somehow.

Or else she was jealous.

The idea struck him as suddenly humorous, and he had to choke back a laugh. Sputtering into his napkin, he looked across the table at Christina. She had her hand on Gracie's head, not with the same tension he'd observed at other times, but calmly, assertively, as she explained to Diana how she'd been helping Eva make friends with the dog.

"Wow," Diana murmured. "I'm impressed."

"You should be, because I sure am." Seth eased back his chair. "Christina, we should get those groceries and head back to the ranch."

She crumpled her napkin onto her empty plate. "Ready whenever you are."

On their way to the exit, Diana called Seth's name. "Will you be at the church chili cook-off next Sunday? You know how you love my dad's chili."

"Probably, if our weekend guests have checked out by then." He set a hand lightly against Christina's waist. "We'll all try to come."

His gesture had the intended effect—on Diana, at any rate. With a smile that held more consternation than cordiality, she replied, "Great. I'll watch for you."

The effect on Christina was more subtle. On the sidewalk out front, she quickened her steps, which instantly put distance between his hand and her back. "I haven't made it to church here yet. Where do you attend?"

"Shepherd of the Hills. It's a little church a few blocks north of the square." Seth checked for traffic before stepping off the curb. "I don't make it as often as I should. It's hard to get away when we have ranch guests on Sunday mornings, so I usually stay home to keep an eye on things."

"I can see how that would be a problem." The judgmental edge had slipped into her tone again.

He tried to bridle his defensiveness. "My grandparents try to get the kids to Sunday school, though. Usually at least one of them can get away."

They were crossing the square now, and Seth's steps slowed as he neared the statue. He could almost feel his dad's eyes on him, could sense the disappointment from a man who put the Lord above all else. What would his dad say, knowing how Seth had all but shut God out of his life after Georgia left him?

After she tried to take away his kids and then got sick and died?

Christina paused several steps ahead. "I thought you were in a hurry to get the shopping done."

"Yeah, right." They crossed to the pickup, and he helped Christina get Gracie into the back seat.

An hour later they arrived at the ranch. Seth dropped Christina at her cabin, then parked in front of the garage and carried the groceries in to Omi.

She glanced up from helping Joseph and Eva spoon mounds of cookie dough onto a baking sheet. "Took you long enough."

"We stopped for coffee at Diana's." Seth dipped a finger into the mixing bowl, then dodged his grandmother's hand slap.

"Good. I'd like for Christina to get to know some folks in town." Omi nudged one of Eva's messy clumps of dough into line with the others. "A little smaller, honey, or they'll all run together."

"But I like them big," Eva said. "Can we take some to Miss Christina when they're all cooked?"

"Sure. After lunch and before your nap." Turning to

check the batch in the oven, Omi frowned at Seth. "I hope you're planning on going to the chili cook-off with us."

"If I can get away."

Omi's eye roll told him what she thought of his reply.

He scoffed. "Somebody's got to make sure our guests get out of here okay."

"They should be gone long before then. The Abbots have a six-hour drive back to Brownsville, and the other families both have early-afternoon flights out of San Antonio." Taking the cookie sheet from the oven, Omi set it on a rack to cool. "Anyway, I bet Christina would love to go. Make sure you invite her."

"Make sure *I* invite her? Why don't you?"

"Oh, you'll probably see her first." Omi winked. "When you and the kids take her a plate of cookies later."

Seth chewed the inside of his lip while he watched his grandmother slide the next batch of cookies into the oven. Her matchmaking efforts were way too obvious. Didn't matter he'd purposely insinuated to Diana earlier that he had something going with Christina. His sole purpose had been to fend off Diana's never-ending hints for a date. He liked her well enough as a friend, but that was as far as it would ever go.

He was growing to like Christina, too. Just not in the way his grandmother might hope. He didn't know if he'd ever be ready for love again. Between his children and his own battered heart, too much was at stake.

"I need to finish up in the barn," Seth said, sliding off the barstool. He circled to his grandmother's side of the counter and leaned in close. "But later, I think you and I need to have a talk—in private."

Chapter Six

The weekend kept Christina busy freshening cabins for the three families who had checked in on Friday. Seth led a trail ride on Saturday morning, and that evening the Petersons hosted another festive barbecue down by the lake, complete with campfire, s'mores, and sing-alongs. Bryan Peterson proved to be quite the guitar player, and when Marie and Seth harmonized to country songs both old and new, Christina hummed along as she offered refills of sweet tea or root beer.

On Sunday morning, she'd just started restocking the maid's cart when a middle-aged couple stepped onto the porch after breakfast. As Bryan walked out with them, the husband said, "You've got a great place here. Next time, we're bringing our grandkids. They'd have a blast."

"Glad you enjoyed yourselves," Bryan replied. "We do aim to please."

"Can't believe you weren't full up, though." The man chuckled. "This must be the best-kept secret in Texas."

Standing out of sight in the workroom doorway, Christina caught Bryan's grimace. It bothered her, too, that the ranch didn't have more business. Serenity Hills was an ideal getaway for families with children.

Although she hated to imagine how much harder she'd be working if the place were booked to capacity.

Bryan offered to help the couple load up their luggage, and while he accompanied them to their cabin, Christina returned to her task. Since all the guests expected to check out by ten, there was little more she needed to do until they vacated their cabins. She sighed. Seth was right—running a guest ranch wasn't exactly conducive to attending Sunday morning worship services, and Christina really missed church.

Footsteps sounded behind her, then Marie spoke. "Leave all that for now, honey. Thought you might want to go to church with me and the kiddos."

"I would love it, more than you'll ever know." Christina almost wept with gratitude. "But I'm in my work clothes. Do I have time to change?"

Marie's gaze swept Christina's pink polo shirt, khaki shorts and sneakers. "You look just fine, sweetie. This is a country church, not the big city."

It helped that Marie was dressed in jeans and a flowered camp shirt. "Okay. Let me just run to grab my purse and Gracie's harness."

A few minutes later, with Gracie buckled between Joseph and Eva in the back seat of the Petersons' SUV, Christina climbed into the passenger seat. Behind the wheel, Marie swiveled to look over her shoulder and clucked her tongue. "If that don't beat all."

Christina followed her gaze to where Eva sat in her booster seat, one hand calmly stroking Gracie's back. A shivery smile stole across Christina's lips. "I have the best dog in the world."

"I think you do."

Yet as relaxed as both children seemed, as they neared the church, Eva's anxiety increased. "Omi, I don't want to go to my class."

"We've talked about this, hon," Marie said patiently. "Omi's always right next door."

"Can Joseph go with me, then?"

Joseph groaned. "I'm too big for your class, Eva. You need to be brave and just go."

Christina glanced back to see a big, fat tear slide down Eva's cheek. To Marie, she whispered, "Maybe Gracie and I could stay with her this time."

"Are you sure?" Marie pulled into a parking spot. "I was going to invite you to my adult Bible study."

"Anything to help."

"Well, it might save her teacher from having to pull me out of class because Eva's crying again."

Christina unbuckled her seat belt. "I've had a lot of experience helping children with separation anxiety. Getting over it is a step-by-step process. Maybe Gracie can be one of those stepping-stones."

Once inside the building, Christina's first challenge was getting Eva to release Marie's hand. "Okay, Eva, give Omi a kiss and say, 'See you after Sunday school.' Then I want you to introduce Gracie and me to your teacher."

Eva balked at first, but Marie stayed strong and leaned down for her kiss. "See you after Sunday school, honey. Go on in with Christina. I need to take Joseph to his class now."

As Christina watched them go, she detected the slightest hesitation in Joseph. He might pretend to be brave, but she'd seen his anxious side more than once. She'd also begun to wonder whether his anxiety stemmed more from his own fears or from protectiveness of his little sister. Neither attitude was healthy, for either of the children.

When Christina introduced herself and Gracie to Eva's Sunday school teacher, the woman expressed only a moment of surprise but then quickly offered her gratitude. She invited Christina to bring Eva and the dog up front, which turned out to be a wise choice since otherwise the children would have spent the entire hour squirming to get a look at Gracie. The teacher even found ways to use Gracie as an example as she taught the class about how the Holy Spirit comes alongside God's children as helper, encourager and comforter.

The children asked lots of questions about Gracie, and Eva gradually warmed to the attention. By the end of class, she seemed a much different child from the scared little girl Christina had walked in with. Her teacher noticed and pulled Christina aside. "Eva has never made it all the way through the Sunday school hour before. You must be great with kids. What did you do before—" With a quick glance at Gracie, she caught herself. "Sorry, I shouldn't ask."

"No, it's all right," Christina answered. "Before my accident, I was a child and family social worker. I love helping children, and I'm hoping I'll eventually be able to return to my career."

The teacher gave Christina's hand a warm squeeze. "I'll pray for that."

In the corridor, they met up with Marie and Joseph. "How'd it go?" Marie asked. Then she took one look at Eva, and her nervous frown turned into a grin. "Guess I know the answer. Can't wait to tell Seth."

Eva tugged on Marie's shirttail. "Omi, I don't want Miss Christina to go away to her job that she had helping other kids. Will you please make her and Gracie stay with us?"

Christina's mouth fell open. She hadn't realized Eva had been paying attention to the conversation with her teacher.

"Eva, honey, you know we can't *make* Miss Christina stay." Marie shot Christina a meaningful glance as she propelled the children toward the sanctuary. "But we sure will enjoy having her around for as long as possible. And personally," she added so only Christina could hear, "I hope that's for a long, long time."

No words formed. Christina didn't realize how unsettled she was growing until Gracie whined and nudged her hand. Walking ahead, Marie didn't notice, and Christina used the moments to consciously calm herself.

What had brought this on? She'd felt perfectly relaxed while sitting with Eva in the Sunday school class. It couldn't have been the simple act of confessing her hope of returning to social work. She'd intended all along for this job to be temporary—just as with Gracie helping Eva, a stepping-stone in her recovery. Christina's goal hadn't changed: to become strong enough emotionally and physically so that she could return to Little Rock and the work she loved.

So, then, was it Eva's declaration about wanting her to stay? It was true, she'd grown attached to two very special children in ways she never could have allowed herself in her role as a social worker. Maybe she should back off a bit, or there could be even bigger problems when the time came for her to leave.

Then a little girl's sweet smile and tiny voice threw all her best intentions out the window. "Are you coming, Miss Christina? I want to sit by you and Gracie in church."

* * *

The combination of old favorite hymns and popular praise songs, along with hearing the Word of God preached by an eloquent but unpretentious pastor, helped Christina settle her thoughts. She found the small but friendly congregation much less overwhelming than the 2,000-member church her family attended in Little Rock. Since recovering from the accident, Christina had taken to worshipping at the church's quieter Saturday evening service so she wouldn't have to face the Sunday morning crowd.

Baby steps.

Not fun when she really wanted to run…straight back to the rewarding career that had been ripped from her grasp the day of the accident.

"Hi, Christine." The brunette from the doughnut shop stood in front of her. "Nice to see you in church."

Fingers twining through Gracie's fur, she tried to smile. "It's Christina, with an *a*."

"I get that all the time, too. People never remember it's Dian-*a*, not Diane." She paused to greet Marie. "Y'all coming to the cook-off?"

"Wouldn't miss it," Marie said. "Your daddy expecting to win again?"

Diana barked a laugh. "If he doesn't, we'll have to listen to him gripe till this time next year! Well, I gotta skedaddle. I'm on the setup committee, and we're starting right after lunch. See y'all later!"

"She'd win the prize for perkiness," Christina muttered, more to herself than Marie.

Gracie's head bobbed beneath her hand.

"Okay, okay, I'm breathing."

Marie studied her with concern. "Too much excitement for one morning?"

"Something like that." Christina massaged her temple, a headache creeping in. "Not sure what's going on with me today. I was feeling really good this morning."

"New church, new faces—it's understandable." Marie aimed the children toward the exit. "Don't mean to pressure you about the chili cook-off, but I do think the more you get to know folks around Juniper Bluff, the more comfortable you'll feel."

"I'm sure you're right." Except Christina couldn't help asking herself exactly how comfortable she wanted to be—how comfortable she *dared* to be—in these new surroundings. She didn't plan on changing sheets and cleaning bathrooms forever.

When they arrived at the ranch, Marie invited Christina to have lunch with the family, but she declined. "I think I'm ready for a little quiet time, but thank you."

"Just don't you start on the guest cabins this afternoon. They'll keep till the morning."

Christina laughed as she helped Gracie from the back seat. "You don't have to tell me twice."

"You rest up, and if you feel like it later, we'll be leaving for the cook-off around four."

Eva tapped Christina's arm. "I want you to go with us. Please?"

How could she resist such a sweet invitation? "We'll see, honey. But I'll definitely need a nap first. How about you?"

Lower lip protruding, Eva wrinkled her brow. "I'm almost getting too big for naps."

"Key word—*almost*," Marie said with a laugh. She latched a hand around each child's shoulder. "Come on, kiddos, let's go see what Opi and Daddy are up to. Have a good rest, Christina. Don't forget—"

"Four o'clock. I'll let you know one way or the other before then." Christina started down the path to her cabin.

As she passed through the copse of trees, Seth's voice rang out behind her. "Christina, wait! We need some help."

Halting, she spun around and instantly recognized the look of worry in Seth's eyes. "What's wrong? What happened?"

Seth hated to ask, and didn't even know if he should risk it, considering Christina's PTSD. But Opi had nearly passed out earlier and scared him silly.

"It's my grandfather," Seth said, catching up to Christina on the path. "One of the guests had a flat this morning, and he helped change the tire. It wasn't until everyone had checked out that I noticed how pale and shaky he was. I'm scared he's going to have a heart attack or something."

"Oh, no! How can I help?"

"You've been so good with the kids. I thought maybe you could keep them occupied for a while."

"Yes, of course. Whatever you need."

"Thanks." Seth palmed the back of his neck. "We're trying to talk my grandfather into letting us take him to the emergency clinic."

"That's probably smart. Does he have a history of heart problems?"

"He's on blood pressure pills." They started toward the house. "But he's being a stubborn old coot, insisting he's fine. Omi's getting on his case right now, and I'm worried the kids will pick up on the tension."

"How about if I make the kids some lunch and take them down to the lake? Then you can——"

Before she could finish, the back door burst open and Omi bustled out. "I've convinced him, Seth. Let's go before he changes his mind."

"Go on," Christina said. "The kids will be fine."

He jogged toward the porch, pausing briefly to send her a grateful smile. Two weeks ago, he'd never have considered leaving Joseph and Eva alone with anyone besides his grandparents. For one thing, the kids would have cried hysterically. For another, he flat didn't trust anyone else to care for his kids the way he did.

But something about Christina...

He gave himself a mental shake. This was no time to dwell on the housekeeper's natural way with children. Or his unnerving attraction to her. While Christina coaxed the kids into the kitchen to help her make lunch, Seth joined his grandmother in the family room, where she strove to keep Opi from changing his mind about the clinic.

"You want to make us all crazy?" Seth asked, manhandling his grandfather out of the recliner. "If you won't do it for yourself, at least think of us. Don't we deserve some peace of mind?"

Opi wavered as he stood. "All right, take it easy. I'll go."

Seth braced his grandfather around the waist. "Can you make it to the pickup?"

"Yes, I can make it to the pickup. I'm not dead yet."

Opi's choice of words corkscrewed through Seth's belly. He and Omi exchanged concerned frowns.

As soon as Seth got his grandparents into the pickup,

he hurried back to the house. He couldn't leave without one last check to make sure the kids would be okay.

He needn't have worried. Joseph and Eva perched on barstools opposite the counter where Christina was adding ingredients to the blender.

"Mango smoothies are my favorite," she said as she plopped in a spoonful of yogurt. "What else should we add?"

"How about peanut butter?" Eva suggested.

"Mmm, great idea! Joseph, can you get it from the pantry?"

Before his son noticed him, Seth slipped quietly out the door. Then, through the screen, he caught Joseph's timid question: "Miss Christina, is Opi going to be okay?"

What happened next brought a clutch to Seth's chest. Christina turned from the counter, wrapped her arms around Joseph and kissed the top of his head. "With your awesome dad looking after him, how could he not be?"

Awesome, huh? Seth couldn't help smiling.

The pickup horn blared, his grandmother's reminder to get a move on. He dashed down the porch steps and climbed in behind the wheel. Ignoring speed limit signs, he made it to town in record time and parked on Main Street in front of the drugstore. The emergency clinic housed inside was the next best thing to driving all the way to Hill Country Memorial in Fredericksburg.

Kelly Nesbit, their nearest neighbor and a nurse practitioner, met them at the check-in desk. "What's going on, Bryan?"

"Felt a little light-headed this morning." He harrumphed as he accepted the clipboard Kelly handed him. "I tried to tell my wife and grandson that's all it is, but they don't believe me."

Omi snatched the clipboard. "I'll take care of this. We'll let Kelly tell us how sick you are."

"I'm not sick," Opi snapped, but to Seth his pallor looked even worse. He'd had to lean on both Seth and Omi to make it from the pickup to the clinic.

Kelly guided him through to the inner office, and Seth followed. He leaned against the wall while Kelly listened to Opi's heart and took his vitals. Her pinched frown told Seth plenty.

Pulling up something at her computer terminal, Kelly asked, "Bryan, have you been taking your blood pressure pills?"

"Most days."

Kelly arched a brow. "How about today?"

Opi's gaze flicked in Seth's direction. "I maybe forgot this morning."

Making notes in her computer file, Kelly said, "I see your cardiologist added a second cholesterol medication at your last visit. Have you had any problems with it?"

Omi had joined them. She handed Kelly the clipboard. "He's been whining around lately with a few more aches and pains."

"Typical of some statins." Kelly perused the form Omi had filled out. "But don't stop or decrease any of your meds without talking to your cardiologist. He might be able to make some adjustments."

Opi's guilty-looking flinch suggested he might have already cut back on those medications. "I'm not scheduled to see the doc again for another couple of months."

"Then you should probably call and move up your appointment." Rising, Kelly started for the door. "Be right back."

Omi huffed and crossed her arms. She looked plenty

mad, but Seth detected a sheen of moisture in her eyes. "You pigheaded old man. How many times do you have to be reminded to take care of yourself? If you were to—" She clamped her lips together and turned away.

"Aw, sweetheart..." Opi tugged her hand free and pulled her down into the chair next to his. He shot a glance at Seth. "How about you leave us alone for a minute, son?"

Exhaling sharply, Seth reached for the doorknob. "Behave yourself, though. I'll be right outside."

As he stepped out, Kelly came around the corner from the pharmacy with a pill container and a small cup of water. "Everything okay in there?"

"They needed a moment. Omi's more shaken up by this episode than she wants to admit." He nodded to the pill. "What's that?"

"A dose of his blood pressure prescription. And I'm serious—he needs to get to his cardiologist ASAP."

"I'll make sure of it." Seth frowned toward the door. "But he'll be okay today?"

"We'll see how fast this kicks in. Can you stay an hour or so while I monitor him?"

"We'll stay as long as it takes."

This was Christina's first time to be on the ranch without at least one of the other adults around, and the place seemed eerily quiet. She'd been able to distract the children with making fruit-and-yogurt smoothies, after which they'd carried their lidded cups and a small container of oatmeal cookies down to the lake. They lunched while watching a family of ducks paddle across the water, but the kids soon grew restless.

As they ambled along the pasture fences to visit the

horses, Joseph grabbed Christina's wrist to look at the time on her watch. "It's almost two o'clock. How much longer before Dad comes back?"

"I'm sure we'll hear something soon." Christina kept her tone light, but her concerns mounted with every passing minute. What if they had to admit Bryan to the hospital? Would Seth and Marie be so distraught that they'd forget to let Christina know what was happening?

As she slipped out her cell phone to make sure she hadn't missed a call, the phone rang in her hand. Seeing Seth's name on the display, she hurriedly pressed the answer button. "Seth? How's Bryan?"

"He's going to be fine…for now, anyway. Forgot to take his meds this morning." As relieved as he sounded, an edge of tension tinged his tone. "How are the kids? Any problems?"

"Everything's fine. They're just hoping you'll be home soon." She cast the children a reassuring smile and whispered, "It's your dad. He says Opi is okay."

"We should only be another hour or so," Seth said. "The nurse is making sure Opi's blood pressure stays down."

Joseph tapped Christina's arm. "Can I talk to him?"

She passed him the phone, then knelt beside Eva while Joseph peppered his dad with more questions.

The moment Christina answered the call, Eva had locked her arm around Gracie's neck. Now, her lower lip trembled, and a fat tear slipped down her cheek. "I want my daddy."

"He'll be home soon, honey, I promise." Christina rubbed the little girl's back, only to be bowled over when Eva let go of Gracie and threw her arms around Christina. The force of that little body clinging to her, the utter abandon with which Eva had entrusted her heart to Christina—it took her breath away, and she hugged back for all she was worth. "Oh, sweetie-pie, it's okay. Everything's going to be okay."

Hanging up with his dad, Joseph returned the phone to Christina, then laid a comforting arm around Eva's shoulders. For several moments the three of them huddled together, and Christina blinked back tears as Joseph offered big-brother words of consolation to his sister— words Christina suspected were as much to reassure himself as Eva.

Then Gracie gave a yip. Prancing on her forepaws, she licked each of their faces in turn, until they broke out into giggles and begged her to stop. Nothing like a little dog slobber to lighten the mood, and even more evidence of Gracie's keen sense of her purpose.

"That's enough, girl!" With a pat to the dog's head, Christina pushed to her feet. "Kids, why don't we head back to the house and finish cleaning up the kitchen. Then we can read a book together until everybody gets home."

The children skipped ahead, giving Christina a little space to gather her thoughts. She was profoundly aware of the confidence placed in her today, not just by Joseph and Eva, but especially by Seth. She'd noticed when he peeked into the kitchen before leaving with his grandparents, but when he slipped out without saying anything, her self-assurance soared in a way she hadn't experienced since before the accident.

She *was* getting stronger, and someday—maybe sooner than she'd dared hope for until now—she might actually be able to return to social work.

Lord, please...please.

"Miss Christina, hurry up!" Eva ran back to clutch Christina's hand.

Once again her heart surged, but this time with an entirely different kind of hopefulness. Like a jolt of electricity, she was hit with the sudden realization that she wanted children of her own one day. She wanted marriage and a family and everything that went with it.

Was it possible? After the accident, the long months in rehab, and the devastating fear that the brain injury would leave her permanently disabled, could she really hope to live a completely normal life again, a life that encompassed both a rewarding career and a loving, close-knit family?

She looked down at the tiny hand gripping hers, the trusting eyes gazing up at her, and realized that whatever professional boundaries she'd resolved to keep had crumbled.

And she didn't care.

Chapter Seven

"No, I do *not* think it's a good idea for you to go to the chili cook-off." Seth glared at his grandfather in the passenger seat as they drove home. Opi's color had definitely improved after he'd taken the forgotten meds, and Kelly promised he was in no immediate danger, but Seth couldn't help worrying.

"Aw, come on, Seth." Opi heaved a groan. "What am I gonna do besides sit in my lawn chair and eat chili? I'll be fine."

"I know you. You don't know the meaning of r-e-s-t. You'll be flitting around the churchyard and yammering with all your pals."

"How about we hog-tie him to his chair?" Omi suggested, and none too kindly. "Or I can sit on him."

Glancing at his grandmother through the rearview mirror, Seth offered a smirk. "You're gonna have to be the one keeping an eye on him. I wash my hands of the old coot."

He didn't mean it, not really, but what was he supposed to do when Opi got so careless with his own health? Seth wasn't ready—would *never* be ready—to lose the man who'd raised him after Daddy died.

As if reading Seth's mind, Opi reached across the console to lay a hand on his arm. "I'll take better care, son, I promise."

Jaw firm, Seth kept his eyes on the road. "See that you do."

At home, Seth's first thought was to get his grandfather inside and plant him in his recliner for a nap. Before they made it as far as the back door, the kids rushed out and waylaid Seth with bear hugs.

"We missed you, Daddy!" Eva scrambled into his arms and locked him in a choke hold.

He loosened her grip enough so that he could breathe. "Missed you, too, sweet thing."

Then it struck him. Eva wasn't crying or panicky. In fact, she was acting downright giggly. He drew his head back for a better look at his bright-eyed little girl, then broke into a smile.

Joseph had transferred his hug to Seth's grandfather. "Come sit in your chair, Opi. Miss Christina made you lemonade and cookies."

"She did?" Opi let Joseph lead him inside. "Then let's not keep her waiting."

Christina stood at the end of the kitchen counter, and Seth smiled his gratitude. The kids seemed plenty anxious to help their great-grandfather get settled in his recliner with his snack, and with Omi overseeing the proceedings, Seth detoured back to the kitchen to offer Christina a more personal thank-you.

She turned from setting the pitcher of lemonade in the fridge. "Oh, would you like a glass?"

"Sounds good." He took a tumbler from the cupboard. "Will you join me?"

"The kids and I just had some. Anyway, I should get

out of your way." She handed him the lemonade pitcher, then started for the door. "Let's go, Gracie."

"Wait." Seth felt the strain of the day catching up with him, and for some crazy reason he didn't want to be alone. Truth be told, he didn't want Christina to leave. Turning so she couldn't read anything into his expression, he filled his glass. Nodding toward the table, he said, "Sit down for a few minutes and tell me how it went with the kids."

She hesitated before taking a seat across from him. "We had a great time." Her smile turned wistful. "Those kids are…very special."

"You don't have to convince me." Eyeing her thoughtfully, Seth sipped his drink. "The kids are different since you got here."

Christina gave a dismissive laugh. "They're just coming out of their shells, that's all."

"It's more than that. Eva's hugging on your dog, both kids are sleeping better at night, and today's the first time I've ever left the kids for a while and didn't come home to find Eva a bundle of tears." He shook his head in disbelief. "How'd you do it?"

"I've just always had a thing for kids." Her glance shifted toward the door. She looked ready to bolt.

Gracie whined and pushed her nose under Christina's elbow.

Seth reached for Christina's other hand, lying on the table. "What is it? What's Gracie sensing?"

"I guess she thinks I'm getting a little anxious."

"And are you?"

"No… Maybe." She chewed her lip. "I said lots of prayers for your grandfather. I'm so relieved he's okay."

"We all are." Seth suspected she held something back,

but he wouldn't press. He slid his hand away and picked up his glass. "Sorry for keeping you. You're probably beat."

"I am, but glad I could help out." One hand on Gracie's back, Christina pushed to her feet.

Seth walked her to the back porch. "By the way, we're still planning on heading over for the chili cook-off later—Opi's insisting. You're welcome to join us if you feel up to it."

She paused on the steps. "Thanks. I'll think about it."

"I'll knock on your door a few minutes before we leave. You can decide then."

Watching her start down the path, Seth had his doubts, and not just about whether she'd go to the cook-off with them. He was beginning to question himself, his absolute aversion to letting another woman into his heart. Because if ever the woman existed who could break down his reserves, it just might be Christina Hunter.

While his grandfather napped in the recliner and Omi stretched out on the sofa, Seth took the kids upstairs to his room. With Joseph and Eva camped out on either side of him in the queen-size bed, he tuned his TV to a baseball game and told the kids the only way he'd even consider taking them to the chili cook-off was if they all rested for an hour or so.

Before he realized he'd fallen asleep, Joseph was shaking him out of a nap-induced stupor. "Come on, Dad, it's time to go."

"Okay, okay." He sat up and scrubbed his palms down his face. "Let me get my boots back on."

Eva bounced on the mattress. "Is Miss Christina coming, too? With Gracie?"

"I don't know yet, hon." Seth wasn't sure he even knew

his own name at the moment. "Y'all run downstairs and see if Omi and Opi are ready to go."

As soon as they bounded out of the room, he stumbled to the bathroom and splashed water on his face. While changing into a fresh shirt, he gazed out the window toward Christina's cabin. Everything looked quiet over there. Maybe she'd rather not be disturbed. It might be better all around if she didn't go along, because every minute he spent with her only lowered his reserves that much more.

With breath-stealing clarity, the dream Joseph had awakened him from flooded his mind. He saw himself loping Tango across a grassy field. A woman rode beside him, her golden ponytail bouncing and her laughter ringing like wind chimes on the morning breeze. He thought it was Georgia at first, except no-nonsense Georgia always said long hair was impractical and kept hers pixie-short.

Then he'd recognized Christina, and as she spurred her horse faster and faster toward a deep, dark forest, his chest had constricted with the fear of losing her. The last thing he remembered before Joseph jolted him awake was calling her name and begging her to stay.

"Dad." Joseph pounded on the door frame. "Omi and Opi are yelling at each other."

"Be right there." Shaking off the unsettling images, Seth grabbed his billfold and keys off the dresser.

Before he made it downstairs, Opi's voice rang out from the hallway. "I will *not* miss Chuck Matthews's prize-winning chili, so just get your purse, woman, and stop nagging."

"Why, you miserable old—"

"Cool it, Omi." Seth gently pulled her aside. "Keep

hounding him and you'll only raise his blood pressure again." He kissed her forehead in a vain attempt to soothe the worry from her furrowed brow. "We'll all keep an eye on him. He'll do fine."

Leaning in for a hug, Omi exhaled sharply. "Thank God we have you, son, or I don't know how we'd keep this place going."

Seth gripped his grandmother's shoulders and looked her squarely in the eye. "This is my home and always will be, and I'll always take care of you and Opi."

Omi didn't often cry, but her eyes glistened with moisture. Straightening, she nodded firmly. "All righty, then, we best go—"

The office phone rang.

"I'll get it," Seth said. "You take Opi and the kids out to the pickup."

Rounding the corner into the office, he snatched up the receiver. "Serenity Hills Guest Ranch."

"Hi, this is Dave Finch from New Braunfels. My family booked a weekend at your place last summer, and we had a ball. This is really last-minute, but we'd like to come over this evening and stay for the whole week, kind of a last blast for the boys before school starts."

Seth vaguely remembered the Finch family and their three rambunctious sons. He winced. "Uh, tonight? Okay. We can put you in cabin four with the loft again. What time should we expect you?"

"Seven thirty or eight at the earliest. We still have some packing to do."

So much for enjoying a leisurely evening at the chili cook-off. Seth took down the Finches' registration information, then went out to break the news to his grandparents.

Omi finished buckling Eva into her booster seat. "Oh, dear. I just sent Joseph over to see if Christina wanted to go to the cook-off with us, but now somebody's got to stay and tidy the cabin."

"We'll take two vehicles," Seth said. "If Christina comes along—"

He looked up to see her rounding the garage with Joseph. When she caught his eye and smiled, his heart flipped.

"She wants to go!" Joseph yelled, jogging to the pickup. Then he glanced back at Gracie. "Uh-oh, can we all fit?"

As Christina and her dog drew near, Seth quickly explained about the last-minute reservation. "I was about to tell Omi we should take two vehicles. You and I can leave the cook-off a little early."

Doubts etched Christina's brow. "I don't mind staying behind. It's work I should have done this morning, anyway."

"Nonsense," Omi stated. "Christina, you and Gracie come ride with me in the SUV. Seth can take Bryan and the kids in the pickup."

Except Seth didn't want Christina riding with Omi. He wanted her right up front in the pickup cab with him. As Omi pushed the button to open the garage door, the memory of Seth's naptime dream invaded. This was a small thing, Christina walking away toward his grandmother's SUV, but combined with the scare Opi had given him and then the dream, it brought back all kinds of emotions he'd vowed never to feel again. He simply couldn't bear to lose one more person he cared about.

And the bald truth was, he was beginning to care about Christina way too much.

* * *

Emotionally and physically drained after the crazy day she'd already had, Christina had fully intended *not* to go to the chili cook-off.

And then Joseph rapped on her door. When she saw the eager anticipation radiating from his dimpled grin, how could she say no? If the socializing grew too overwhelming, surely she could find a quiet corner and escape for a while.

At least now she could look forward to leaving the gathering earlier rather than later.

Leaving with Seth. The two of them. Alone.

From the back seat of Marie's SUV, Gracie stretched her chin across Christina's shoulder and nuzzled her ear. The dog had acted almost as anxious as Joseph for Christina to grab her purse and hurry out the door. *What do you know that I don't, girl?*

Or didn't want to admit?

She tuned in to what Marie was chattering about, mostly the woman's worries over her husband's health and how she planned to call Bryan's cardiologist first thing in the morning.

"Can't tell men anything," Marie said with a huff. "Always gotta do things their own way in their own time. Well, not *this* time, let me tell you. I've invested too many years in that man to see him acting like a nincompoop and taking chances like this."

The rant continued all the way to the church, with Christina mainly smiling and nodding while keeping her own emotions in check by reaching back to stroke Gracie's head. She understood Marie's need to vent and knew the angry words only reflected the woman's deep love for her husband…and her fear of losing him.

Fragments of other conversations sifted through Christina's thoughts. She hadn't been aware of much during her hospital stay, but she retained vague memories of her mother's barely muted tirades, sometimes against the driver of the dump truck, but more often against the shotgun-wielding lowlife responsible for Christina's frantic flight to save little Haley Vernon. It was anger born of helplessness, a mother's stark realization that there was nothing she could have done to prevent what happened that day.

And nothing she could do to change the course of her daughter's recovery except try to be there every moment of every day until she nearly drove Christina mad with her hovering.

It was why Christina had come all the way to Juniper Bluff, Texas—and why she'd stayed, despite her initial misgivings about Seth, and despite the labor-intensive work so far removed from the career she'd trained for.

Yet now, not even two weeks since her arrival, she felt an unexpected sense of belonging. This family had accepted her, included her, made her feel almost like one of them. Was she being fair to them, or to herself, when she harbored hopes of returning to Little Rock the moment she felt physically and emotionally ready?

Joining the throng at the chili cook-off, Christina was soon greeted by many of the same friendly folks she'd met at church that morning. She fielded plenty of questions about Gracie's blue service dog vest, and naturally every child who came near wanted to "pet the pretty puppy." Joseph and Eva took a protective stance, warming Christina's heart as they proudly explained that Gracie shouldn't be bothered while on duty. However, once Christina had settled into a lawn chair with the plastic tumbler of sweet tea Seth brought her, she didn't mind inviting children over a few at a time to lavish the dog with affection.

When people began lining up for bowls of chili, Joseph and Eva each grabbed one of Christina's hands and led her to the serving tables. "Daddy and Opi like Mr. Matthews's chili best, but it burns my mouth," Joseph said. "Me and Eva like Pastor Terry's."

Christina accepted the serving tray Joseph handed her. "Then I'll have some of Pastor Terry's, too."

Behind her, Seth's chuckle rumbled. "What—you can't handle five-alarm chili?"

"I prefer not to scorch my taste buds. Or my stomach lining." Giving her ponytail a flip, she followed Joseph and Eva.

After the pastor ladled hearty servings into each of their bowls, the kids led Christina to one of the long tables. Bryan already sat at one end, and by the time Christina settled into a chair, Marie and Seth ambled over and set down their trays across from Christina.

They'd barely started eating when Diana Matthews peered over Seth's shoulder, her cheek brushing his. "I hope that's my daddy's chili in your bowl."

Looking slightly uncomfortable, Seth slanted his head away from hers. "You know he always gets my vote."

She pulled out the chair next to his. "I heard about your little scare this afternoon." Leaning around Seth, she asked, "How are you feeling, Mr. Peterson?"

With a good-natured snicker, Bryan answered, "I'll feel a lot better when all you womenfolk quit fussing over me."

"But we love fussing over our honeys." Diana tucked

her fingers around Seth's biceps. "Isn't that right, Christina?"

This was getting a bit too awkward. Christina edged her chair away from the table. "I think I'm ready for seconds. Would you excuse me?"

Seth stood abruptly, Diana's hand falling away. "Mind if I tag along? I need a tea refill."

But instead of detouring to the beverage table, Seth accompanied Christina to the serving line. While she waited for the pastor to fill her bowl, she cast Seth a curious glance. "Thought you needed more iced tea."

"Not really." He grimaced. "Just needed a break from Diana."

"She does seem to have a thing for you."

"We're friends. That's all."

Not the message Christina was getting, at least from Diana. Retrieving her bowl, she started back to the table, then had second thoughts. Pausing in front of Seth, she said, "This has been really fun, but I'm verging on social overload. I'll wait for you by your pickup, okay?"

"I've about had it, too. I'll be right behind you after I say my goodbyes."

Before Christina could argue that he didn't have to cut his time short on her account, he jogged away. Finding an out-of-the-way spot at the corner of the church building, she finished her bowl of chili and then deposited the bowl in a waste receptacle. A few minutes later, Seth strode toward her with two frosty water bottles.

"Thought you might need this for the road," he said, handing her one. "Ready to go?"

With Gracie secured in the back seat, Seth pulled out of the parking lot. As he drove through town, Christina cast him an appraising glance. He seemed as relieved as she was to escape the crowd…or maybe just the attentions of one overly zealous admirer. A tease in her tone, Christina said, "Anytime life gets too stressful for you, I'm happy to share my dog."

He shot her a grin, and the tension lines around his eyes and mouth began to soften. "Might have to take you up on that."

When they turned off Main Street, Christina smirked as they neared the spot where she'd first met Seth. "Oh, look, here's our special place. Rescued any turtles lately?"

Seth surprised Christina by hitting the brakes and steering the pickup to the curb. He shifted to face her, his expression growing serious. "I hope you've forgiven me for how I acted that day—about Gracie, I mean. She's a terrific dog, and I was an ignorant jerk."

Lips twisted to one side, Christina tapped a finger on her chin. "Yes, yes, yes…and no."

Seth quirked a brow. "Huh?"

"Yes, I've forgiven you. Yes, Gracie is most certainly a terrific dog. And yes, you showed your ignorance that day. But I'd never stoop so low as to call you a jerk." She winced. "Well, not to your face, anyway."

Laughter burst from Seth's throat. "Nobody could ever accuse you of holding back the truth."

She kept her smile in place, but the little detail she'd kept from him at his grandparents' request now churned in her belly and made her wish she hadn't downed the second helping of chili. Laying a hand on her stomach, she reached for her water bottle.

He tilted his head. "You feeling okay?"

"Guess I ate too much." She took several sips of water. "We should get going. I still have a cabin to clean."

"Don't worry, I'll help." Glancing over his left shoulder, Seth pulled onto the road, then looked back at Christina with a wink. "I was thinking we should put up a marker back there to commemorate the day you came into my—" Blinking rapidly, he cleared his throat. "That is, when the kids and I first met you. Because you've really made a difference in our lives."

"I'm just glad I've been able to help." Then, to lighten the moment, she added, "Actually, it probably wouldn't hurt to erect a Turtle Crossing sign so future turtle-rescuing do-gooders don't get rear-ended."

"Good idea." Seth's easy laugh warmed her. When he reached across the console to give her hand a quick squeeze, a whole new batch of feelings spiraled through her chest.

This was crazy. *She* was crazy to imagine for a minute that this could ever be anything more than friendship. In fact, she'd be better off remembering Seth was her employer and her job at Serenity Hills was only a means to an end.

Gracie stretched a paw between the seats and yipped softly.

Seth glanced over. "What's she telling you?"

"Probably that she's ready to get home. It's been a long day for her, too." It was as close to the truth as Christina dared admit, when she knew perfectly well her own tumultuous thoughts had pricked Gracie's senses.

They drove the rest of the way in silence. Seth parked in front of the garage and helped Christina get Gracie out of the back seat.

"Thanks for taking me to the cook-off." Christina absently massaged the hip that sometimes stiffened up. "And thanks for bringing me back early. Guess I'd better get cleaning."

"I told you I'd help. It'll go twice as fast with both of us working."

"You really don't have to—Gracie, stop!" Either the dog really thought Christina's emotions were on overload, or she was just being a pest.

Seth laughed. "I think she *wants* you to accept my help."

"Okay, fine." At her dog's next insistent nudge, Christina pushed back. "I get the message, girl—"

Gracie shoved again, throwing her off balance and straight into Seth's chest.

"Easy there." Seth steadied her in his solid embrace, his surprised breath warm against her face.

Nerves aflame, Christina kept her eyes lowered. "I don't know what's gotten into that dog."

"I think I do." Seth's tone had grown husky, and now Christina couldn't keep herself from peering into his shadowed gaze. Half-lidded eyes, dark and intense, revealed his inner struggle with emotions he clearly resisted.

She knew those feelings well. Her hands clamped down on his forearms. "Seth, please…"

"This is crazy, I know." Inch by inch, he inclined his head toward hers. "But there's something about you. Something I can't—"

At the rumble of tires on gravel, Christina jerked away, her heart galloping. Where was her dog when she needed her?

Seth's chest heaved, and the look he shot Christina spoke both his regret and his relief, because he had to know as well as she did that they'd just been saved from crossing a bridge of no return.

Chapter Eight

Almost kissing Christina? *What had he been thinking?*

Scratch that, because Seth's brain must have gone on vacation about the time Christina fell into his arms. If the Finches hadn't driven up at that exact moment, he could have made the second-worst mistake of his life.

The first being the day he let Georgia leave with their children.

Except thinking of Christina as a mistake went against everything in him. He was attracted to her, no use denying it, and a tiny but growing corner of his heart yearned to find out if something more could come of these feelings.

No time to dwell on the possibilities now, though, not with a cabin to clean and three rowdy boys stampeding around the ranch like a herd of broncs. While Christina readied the cabin with clean sheets and towels, Seth showed the Finch family inside to the reception desk and got them signed in. They apologized for arriving earlier than expected and said they didn't mind hanging out until their accommodations were ready. Soon they'd provided Seth with a long list of activities they wanted

YOUR PARTICIPATION IS REQUESTED!

Dear Reader,

Since you are a lover of our books – we would like to get to know you!

Inside you will find a short Reader's Survey. Sharing your answers with us will help our editorial staff understand who you are and what activities you enjoy.

To thank you for your participation, we would like to send you up to 4 books and 2 gifts – **ABSOLUTELY FREE!**

Enjoy your gifts with our appreciation,

Pam Powers

SEE INSIDE FOR READER'S SURVEY

Get up to 4 Free Books!

Romance ⟩⟨ **Suspense**

We'll send you 2 Free Books from each series you choose plus 2 Free Gifts!

Try **Love Inspired® Romance Larger-Print** books featuring Christian characters facing modern-day challenges.

Try **Love Inspired® Suspense Larger-Print** novels for stories about Christian characters facing challenges to their faith... and lives.

Or **TRY BOTH!**

YOUR READER'S SURVEY
"THANK YOU" FREE GIFTS INCLUDE:

▶ **2 lovely surprise gifts**   ▶ **Up to 4 FREE books**

PLEASE FILL IN THE CIRCLES COMPLETELY TO RESPOND

1) What type of fiction books do you enjoy reading? (Check all that apply)
- ○ Suspense/Thrillers ○ Action/Adventure ○ Modern-day Romances
- ○ Historical Romance ○ Humor ○ Paranormal Romance

2) What attracted you most to the last fiction book you purchased on impulse?
- ○ The Title ○ The Cover ○ The Author ○ The Story

3) What is usually the greatest influencer when you <u>plan</u> to buy a book?
- ○ Advertising ○ Referral ○ Book Review

4) How often do you access the internet?
- ○ Daily ○ Weekly ○ Monthly ○ Rarely or never

YES! I have completed the Reader's Survey. Please send me 2 FREE books and 2 FREE gifts (gifts are worth about $10 retail) from each series selected below. I understand that I am under no obligation to purchase any books, as explained on the back of this card.

Select the series you prefer (check one or both):

❏ **Love Inspired® Romance Larger-Print** (122/322 IDL GMRG)

❏ **Love Inspired® Suspense Larger-Print** (107/307 IDL GMRG)

❏ **Try Both** (122/322/107/307 IDL GMRT)

FIRST NAME   LAST NAME

ADDRESS

APT.#   CITY

STATE/PROV.   ZIP/POSTAL CODE

LI-817-SCT17

READER SERVICE—**Here's how it works:**

▼ If offer card is missing write to: Reader Service, P.O. Box 1341, Buffalo, NY 14240-8531 or visit www.ReaderService.com ▼

BUSINESS REPLY MAIL

FIRST-CLASS MAIL   PERMIT NO. 717   BUFFALO, NY

POSTAGE WILL BE PAID BY ADDRESSEE

READER SERVICE
PO BOX 1341
BUFFALO NY 14240-8571

NO POSTAGE
NECESSARY
IF MAILED
IN THE
UNITED STATES

to plan, including riding lessons, trail rides, swimming, fishing and lakeside barbecues.

This was going to be one busy week, probably a good thing because there'd be plenty to keep Seth's mind *on* the ranch guests and *off* the charmingly fascinating housekeeper he was trying hard not to fall for—and failing miserably.

Despite his best avoidance measures, his path often crossed with Christina's over the next several days as they saw to the guests' needs. Things got even busier when a young couple and a family of four made reservations for the weekend.

On Thursday morning, as Seth headed out to the barn to get horses ready for the Finches' daily trail ride, he glimpsed Christina struggling to push the maid's cart up the hill. The grimace twisting her face, along with her obvious limp, told him she was hurting. He did a quick about-face and jogged over.

"Here, let me." Easing the handle from her grip, he pushed the cart the rest of the way to the workroom.

She trudged in behind him, rubbing her hip. "Thanks. Not sure I could have made it if you hadn't come to my rescue."

"Bad, huh?" Seth guided her to a folding chair. "Would it help to prop your foot on something?"

"No, I just need to stretch through the cramp." Extending her leg, she closed her eyes and took several slow breaths.

Seth looked down to see Gracie sitting at his feet. Those big brown eyes staring up at him seemed to say, *Do something, you idiot.*

He glared at the dog. "You think you're so smart, don't you?"

Christina's eyes popped open. "What?"

"Oh, uh, not you. I mean, obviously you're very smart. I mean, *really* smart, not—" Since when did grown men babble? He shot Christina a sheepish grin. "I was talking to the dog."

Looking a little less pained, Christina called Gracie over and scratched her behind the ears. "Are you pestering Seth? What is going on with you lately, girl?"

"I think she's trying to tell me we've been working you too hard." That was his story and he was sticking by it. Turning his back on the woman who'd started showing up in his dreams way too often, he began transferring towels and sheets to the laundry collection bin.

Christina stepped up beside him and gathered an armful of damp towels. "You don't have to do that. Aren't you taking the Finches on another trail ride this morning?"

"Rafael's getting the horses saddled. I've got time." *Idiot.* She'd given him the perfect out and he opted not to take it. He studied what looked like a chocolate stain on a pillowcase. "Looks like the Finch boys are snacking in their beds again."

"Figures. There were several candy bar wrappers in the wastebasket." Tossing in another towel, Christina groaned. "I love kids, but those boys have run me ragged this week."

"Three more days and they're gone. Think you can survive?"

"Do I have a choice?"

Gracie poked her nose between them and whined.

Christina huffed. "Honestly, girl. When we get back to Little Rock—" Flicking Seth an embarrassed glance, she snapped her mouth shut.

His chest deflated. "I get it. Omi told me this was an

interim job for you, so I know you hope to go back to…
whatever you were doing before."

"Yes, that's the plan." Christina dropped the last of
the laundry into the bin, then marched over to the supply shelf. While methodically referring to the notebook
she pulled from her pocket, she restocked the cart with
an assortment of travel-size soaps, shampoos and lotions.

"I still don't know what you used to do." Seth set a
stack of clean towels on the cart. "But I'm guessing it involved kids somehow. What was it, a day care? Kinder-
garten teacher?"

"Um, no, not exactly." Fingers coiled in Gracie's ruff,
she straightened. "Shouldn't you be heading out on your
ride?"

Seth studied her through slitted eyes. He was about
to press for the answers she seemed so reluctant to give,
when three freckle-faced boys tumbled through the door.

"Hey, Seth." Bobby Finch, the oldest, swept a hank
of red hair off his sweaty forehead. "Are you coming or
not?"

"Be right there. Don't forget your helmets." When
they'd taken their roughhousing outside again, he turned
to tell Christina he'd see her later, only she had her cell
phone to her ear.

"I'm doing great, Mom." She wiggled her fingers at
Seth. "Sure, I can talk for a few minutes."

With a lopsided smile, he waved back, then headed
out to the barn. About time he got his head on straight
where Christina Hunter was concerned.

Over the course of the week, the Finch kids had turned
into pretty decent riders. As boisterous as they could be
when chasing each other around the ranch or splashing in
the lake, once they climbed into the saddle, they settled

right down. Seth knew from years of being around horses how calming they could be. He recalled the framed words of Winston Churchill that hung over the registration desk: "There is something about the outside of a horse that is good for the inside of a man."

He supposed the same basic truth held for what Gracie did for Christina.

And maybe Christina's good for you like that, too?

Except she made him feel anything but settled. In fact, it had been awhile since he'd felt this particular kind of completely *un*settled.

"No, Mom, I haven't decided yet how much longer I'll be working here." Christina carried her phone outside where she could catch the morning breeze. And, okay, where she could catch a glimpse of Seth Austin on horseback.

"But you promise you're feeling well? Not overdoing?" Mom had slipped into her worried-mother voice.

"I told you, I'm fine." The nagging ache in her hip said otherwise, but Christina didn't dare mention it.

"I ran into Lindsey Silva at the supermarket the other day. She asked about you."

Lindsey had been Christina's supervisor at Child Protective Services. "That's nice. How are things going at the department?"

"They miss you, naturally. Lindsey said if you ever feel like you're ready to come back…"

Seth and his riders, including Eva perched up front with him and Joseph riding Spot, headed toward the lake, and Christina stepped to the end of the garage for a better view. She'd rather be out there with them right now instead of skirting difficult topics with her mother. "If you see Lindsey again, tell her I said hi. I should go, Mom. Still have some work to finish."

Her mother said a reluctant goodbye. Tucking the phone into her pocket, Christina heaved a sigh and tore her gaze from the riders now making their way along the hillside trail.

As she started back to the workroom, Marie called to her from the porch. "Got a minute, hon? Need to talk to you about something."

"Sure. What's up?"

Marie motioned Christina inside, where she led her down the hall to the office and quietly closed the door.

Insides quivering, Christina reached for her dog. "This looks serious. I hope I haven't messed up somehow."

"Oh, no, not at all." Marie plopped into one of the side chairs and absently pointed Christina to the other. "Sorry, a lot on my mind this week. You know I took Bryan to see his doc yesterday."

"Yes, how did it go?"

"Doc made some adjustments to his meds and says he's doing pretty good, all things considered." Marie's mouth flattened. "Except he has to cut back on the stress."

Christina had a feeling she knew where this was going. "The doctor wants him to retire?"

"You got it." Marie's eyes glistened. "I don't know what to do, Christina. The ranch is Bryan's whole life. If he has to give it up, I'm afraid that'll be what kills him."

"Isn't there a happy medium? Can't Seth assume more of the management responsibilities?"

"He's doing all he can already, on top of being the best dad he can be to those two little ones." With a shake of her head, Marie rose and paced to the window. "I'm thinking our only choice is to make a clean break. Sell the ranch and move away from Juniper Bluff. If I could convince Bryan to take up golf or fishing, anything to keep him active without stressing him out…"

She didn't sound convinced, only desperate, and Christina didn't know how to help. She joined Marie at the window and slid an arm around her waist. "I'm so sorry. I wish I could do something."

"Thanks, honey." Marie gave her a quick hug. "I just thought you should know. The future's looking too uncertain, and I wouldn't want you to feel obligated to stay if you can find work somewhere else. Leastways, maybe this'll get you back to Little Rock and your career sooner."

Suddenly torn, Christina chewed her lip. Her mother's mention of Lindsey Silva had stirred a restlessness to hurry things along. She was tired of being held captive by her injuries from the auto accident. The aching hip she could deal with, but the effects of head trauma—headaches, anxiety, roller-coaster emotions, occasional forgetfulness—had sidelined her much too long. She grew increasingly eager to get back to the life the accident had stolen from her.

But then the sense of belonging she'd admitted to a few days ago—those feelings were strong, too. The Petersons, Seth and the children had begun to seem as much like family as her own mother and father. In some ways even more so, because here she was treated like a capable adult, not a recovering invalid.

Well, except for times like this morning, when she pushed herself too hard and Seth came to her rescue.

She gave Marie another squeeze. "You're right, we don't know what the future holds. But if and when I decide it's time to move on, I'll give you plenty of notice. Until then, I'm here to help in any way I can."

Nodding mutely, Marie grabbed a tissue from the box

on the desk. After blowing her nose, she cast Christina a misty-eyed smile. "I've said it before and I'll say it again— God brought you to us for a reason, and I'm thanking Him for it every single day."

Excusing herself to get back to work, Christina had to pause in the hallway to dab away a tear of her own.

By the time she finished the morning chores, her stomach was demanding lunch. At her cabin, she made a ham-and-cheese sandwich and a tumbler of iced tea, then took the meal outside and plopped down in the red porch chair. Gracie stretched out across the floor with her chin resting on the toe of Christina's sneaker.

She'd almost finished her sandwich when the *clop-clop* of horses' hooves drew her attention to the lane.

"Thought we'd come by and say hi," Seth called from atop Tango.

Joseph rode up beside him. "You should have come with us today, Miss Christina. We saw an armadillo and a baby copperhead on the trail."

Christina flinched. "I hope not at the same time."

"No, we saw the armadillo first. It had a hole by some big rocks. The copperhead was up the hill a ways."

"Sounds...fun." Swallowing her last bite of sandwich, Christina rose and carried her iced tea to the porch rail. "Where's the rest of the crew?"

Seth rode closer. "Dropped the Finch family at the barn. Rafael's helping them untack." He cast her a concerned frown from beneath the rim of his Stetson. "You doing okay?"

So much for being treated like a capable adult. "When I can't do my job, I'll let you know."

The firm set of his jaw made her regret her bristly tone. "Sorry for caring," he muttered. "It's just that earlier—"

"You're right, and I'm sorry." She strove for a light laugh. "Can we just blame it on those rowdy Finch boys?"

Seth laughed, too. "I think we can safely blame this whole crazy week on the Finch boys."

Well, maybe not *everything*. But it wasn't Christina's place to mention what Seth's grandmother had confided earlier, and especially not in front of Joseph and Eva. What would happen to Seth and the kids if his grandparents decided to sell Serenity Hills?

Seth's saddle leather creaked as he shifted his weight. "I was thinking, since the Finches are driving over to Fredericksburg for dinner tonight and it'll be quiet around here, maybe you'd like a break before the weekend guests check in tomorrow."

"A quiet evening sounds exactly like what I—" Suddenly it dawned on her what he might be asking. Her heart gave a nervous thud. "Um, did you have something in mind?"

"There's a little Mexican food place on the edge of town. Best enchiladas between here and San Antonio."

"I love enchiladas, if they're not too spicy."

"Luis will make them as mild as you like." Seth's lips twitched in a hesitant grin. "Pick you up at six?"

Christina glanced down as Gracie nuzzled her hand. "I, um…"

"See, she's telling you it's okay."

"So now you speak dog?"

"I'm learning." Seth's chuckle shot prickles of warmth up Christina's spine. "Seriously, you'd better do what she tells you, or you might find something unpleasant in your shoe tomorrow morning."

She smirked. "I'll keep that in mind."

"All right, then, see you at six." With a tip of his hat, Seth kicked his horse into a trot.

As Christina watched Seth and his children ride away, she gave her head a frustrated shake. This was not supposed to happen. And yet she couldn't seem to do a thing about it, because the more time she spent with Seth, the more she began to imagine a different kind of life. She still wasn't clear on what exactly that life entailed, but she did know that someday she wanted to experience the joy—the *normalcy*—of love, marriage and children of her own.

"How many times do I have to tell you? It's *not* a date." Seth slapped his Stetson on the kitchen counter. He was glad the kids had gone upstairs to their rooms for an afternoon rest.

"You asked her out to dinner." Grinning over her shoulder, Omi pounded a slab of round steak with an aluminum meat tenderizer. "If it looks like a duck and quacks like a duck…"

Seth figured he should be glad his grandmother wasn't using the gadget to "tenderize" his thick head. "I just thought it would do Christina good to get away from the ranch for a while. She's been going nonstop ever since the Finches checked in."

"Mmm-hmm." Omi laid down the meat tenderizer, then washed and dried her hands. With a meaningful smile curling her lips, she crossed the kitchen to lay her warm palm against Seth's cheek. "Honey, it's okay to let yourself care for someone. And I can't think of a nicer person to let into your heart than Christina."

Covering her hand, he lowered it to his chest and gave a squeeze. "Yes, I like Christina. But I'm in no rush, okay?"

"No rush?" Omi scoffed. "It's been three years, and in

my opinion, that's two years too long. Those kids need a mother. You need a—"

"Don't say it, Omi." Seth swallowed the bitter taste of regret creeping into his throat.

"I *will* say it, whether you want to hear it or not." Clasping his hand with both of hers, she gave it a hard shake. "Seth Austin, you need to take your wounded heart off the shelf and teach it how to love again."

With a pained sigh, he lowered his head. "And exactly how do I do that?"

"Well, like you've been doing ever since Christina came into our lives. You get to know her a little bit at a time. You start trusting her with your children." Omi tweaked his chin, her flinty gaze boring into his. "You take her out for Mexican and you treat her like a lady and you call it what it is—a *date*."

Giving a snort, she whirled around to finish preparing the steak she'd been hammering into submission.

So he was going on a date. *You hear that, heart of mine?*

It gave a little thump, and he wasn't sure if the response was gratitude or panic.

Panic. Definitely panic. Because Seth had been making all kinds of dangerous moves lately. Maybe he needed a dog like Gracie of his own to sound the alert before he lost his cool.

On his way upstairs, he passed the office door and glimpsed his grandfather at the desk. Opi had definitely seemed better the last few days, and Seth was relieved the report from the cardiologist had been encouraging. Still, Opi's troubled look as he studied something on the computer screen didn't bode well.

Seth tapped on the open door and stepped into the office. "Everything okay?"

Opi looked up with a half smile. "Oh, sure, just going over the accounts."

"And? How're we doing?"

"Better than this time last year. Not as good as I'd like." Opi fingered a stack of bills, the one on top from the feed store. "I'm thinking about selling a couple of horses. The way business has been, we could easily get by with fewer."

Seth couldn't argue the point. He sank into a chair opposite his grandfather. "Danny and Sugarbear are getting up in years, but they're also the gentlest mounts for greenhorns. I've been wondering about Cinnamon. She spooks too easily."

Opi nodded his agreement. "You still planning on breeding Tango soon?"

"Hope so. Doc Ingram knows a rancher over toward Bandera with a real nice stallion. Need to talk to him about the fee."

At the mention of money, Opi's jaw muscles clenched. He looked back at the computer screen. "Don't forget, we're gonna need a new roof on the barn before winter. Plus we talked about doing some updates in the cabins."

"I can do the roofing. All we'll need is materials. We can put off refurbishing the cabins for another year or so, can't we?"

"Not if we want to keep our repeat business and get some referrals." Opi shuddered. "Hate to think what cabin four's gonna look like after the Finches check out."

Seth cringed, as much from picturing the damage those boys could do as from seeing what money worries were doing to his grandfather. He came around the desk to rest a hand on Opi's shoulder. "Go play a game with the kids or something. Let me work on the bills for a while."

When his grandfather tried to argue, Seth grabbed

the back of the chair and rolled it away from the computer. He lifted Opi bodily and pointed him toward the door. "Out, I said."

Grumbling under his breath, Opi stomped from the room.

Seth was no stranger to keeping the books but typically left this side of the business to his grandparents.

Well, no more. Opi and Omi weren't getting any younger, and if Seth had any hopes of keeping Serenity Hills going after they retired, he'd better get a firm handle on every aspect of running the guest ranch. He spent the next hour figuring out which bills to pay now and which he could put off a while longer. No wonder his grandfather had trouble keeping his blood pressure down.

Satisfied he'd handled everything urgent and feeling more educated about where the ranch finances stood, Seth eased his chair back. With a tired groan, he pressed his thumbs into the spaces beneath his eyebrows for a brisk massage. He checked the time and decided he'd better make quick work of barn chores before getting cleaned up for this so-called *date* he'd arranged with Christina.

As he started to rise, his glance fell to the file drawer. If Omi really did want Seth to get to know Christina better, shouldn't he learn a little more about her background? Anyway, he had as much right as his grandparents to look at personnel files.

Then why did he feel so guilty?

His hand lingered over the drawer handle. Before he could talk himself out of it, he yanked open the drawer and thumbed through the folders. With a furtive glance toward the door, he laid Christina's folder on his lap and pulled out her application form.

When he read *child and family social worker* under

previous employment, a sickening flood of memories engulfed him. No wonder his grandmother had been so close-mouthed about the subject. She knew as well as anyone what Seth had gone through in the battle for his children.

Hearing footsteps, he shoved the folder back into the drawer and eased it shut. Seconds later, his grandmother peeked in. "Opi said you threw him out." She cast him a wink and a grateful smile. "How's it going?"

"All handled." Teeth clenched, he fought to hold in the torrent of emotions raging through him.

Omi narrowed her gaze. "What's wrong, Seth?"

It took his last ounce of willpower to keep his voice even. "Why didn't you tell me?"

For a full two seconds her eyes darted in a look of confusion. Then her lids fell shut, and she breathed out slowly. "You looked at the personnel file."

"You had to know I'd find out sooner or later."

"Yeah, well, it was the 'later' I was counting on. Hopefully after you'd had a chance to know and like Christina for who she is."

"Who she is, is a social worker, Omi. A *social worker*!" Seth sat back so hard that the chair rammed into the credenza behind him. "How can I trust a single thing she says now? For all I know, she's taking notes on what a lousy dad I am so she can get the kids removed."

"For crying out loud, Seth Austin, would you listen to yourself?" Both hands braced on the desk, Omi leaned toward him, her eyes shooting daggers. "In case you haven't noticed, your daughter isn't afraid of dogs anymore, and your son isn't near as clingy as he was. Tell me one single thing Christina's done that's been a threat to you or the kids."

Made me almost brave enough to risk my heart again, he didn't say. And that alone was plenty threatening.

Chapter Nine

It was six ten and no sign of Seth. Christina paced her narrow porch and wondered if they'd had a miscommunication. "Pick you up at six?" he'd said, *pick you up* being the operative words. Or was he waiting at his truck, expecting Christina to meet him there?

She frowned down at Gracie, all set to go in her blue vest and car harness. "What do you think, girl? Should we walk over or keep waiting?"

Relaxing on her haunches, tongue hanging out like she didn't have a care in the world, Gracie didn't budge.

"Okay, smarty-pants, since you seem to know more about what's going on lately than I do, I guess we wait."

Christina was about to plop down in the metal porch chair when she heard the rumble of tires coming up the lane. Moments later, Seth's maroon pickup stopped in front of her cabin. He shut off the motor, then climbed out and opened the rear door. Without saying a word, he strode over to take Gracie's leash and boosted the dog into the back seat.

Unsure what to make of Seth's silent treatment, Christina edged around him to buckle Gracie in. "Where are the kids?" she asked, surprised they hadn't come along.

"With my grandparents." Barely looking at her, Seth walked her around to the passenger side and pulled open her door.

With one foot on the running board, Christina peered up at him. "I can tell something's bothering you. If you'd rather not go, it's okay."

He exhaled loudly through his nostrils. "Just get in before I change my mind."

A panicky feeling gripped her chest. "Seth—"

"We'll talk, I promise." With a hand at her elbow, he guided her into the seat, then firmly closed the door.

Gracie whimpered and stretched forward to lick Christina's ear. She caressed the dog's head. "Yeah, girl, I know. Something's really wrong."

Seth buckled in behind the wheel, then backed around and headed out toward the road. The grim set of his jaw made Christina's fingers tighten around the edge of her seat. She wished he'd say something—*anything*.

After they'd driven a mile or so, she tried again. "Please, Seth, tell me what's going on."

His Adam's apple made a painful-looking path up and down his throat. "I was going to save this until we got to the restaurant and could talk face-to-face, but obviously that plan isn't working." He shot her a steely glance. "Why didn't you tell me you were a social worker?"

Icy-hot blades sliced through Christina's abdomen. Her lower lip trembled as she forced out her reply. "Because your grandparents asked me not to. They told me what happened with your children and the custody battle." She wanted desperately to reach across the space between them and somehow convince him she'd never have betrayed his trust that way. "What happened to you and the kids was cruel and unfair. I'd like to believe the social worker made an honest mistake, that she completely misjudged the situation, but the truth is I don't know. My only defense is that we're all only human, acting on our training and best instincts in any given situation."

Seth's knuckles whitened on the steering wheel. "Well, her instincts were all wrong in *this* situation."

With nothing else she could say, Christina shifted deeper into the seat and clasped her arms across her waist. She wanted to ask why Seth hadn't just confronted her at the ranch instead of putting them both through this pretense of going out for dinner. Clearly, she was the last person he wanted to be with right now. She wished she could crawl in the back seat with Gracie, bury her face in the dog's cool fur and forget this conversation ever happened.

The pickup slowed, and Seth turned into a crowded gravel parking area outside a long stucco building. Brightly colored murals adorned the walls—dancers in traditional Mexican dress; a mariachi band in striped serapes; saguaro cacti and lush flowers in vibrant shades of red, orange and blue. A sign over the entrance read Casa Luis.

Seth pulled to a stop at the end of a row of cars. Long seconds passed before he exhaled slowly and said, "I guess I should ask if you still want to go in."

Confused and just a little bit angry now, Christina muttered, "You did kind of put a damper on the evening."

He slapped the steering wheel. "If you'd just told me—"

"Then what?" Christina whirled on him. "You'd have never let your grandmother hire me in the first place? Oh, sure, that would've really helped. You'd still have a little girl scared of dogs and a son who can hardly stand for you to be out of his sight. Not to mention you'd probably have ended up hiring a crotchety old hag with purple hair and no teeth, and just imagine the scare she'd put in your ranch guests."

As she spoke, Seth slowly swiveled his head to stare at her, his brows drawing together in disbelief. Jaw dropping, he released something between a groan and a laugh. Then his gaze softened, and the beginnings of a reluctant smile skewed his lips. "Yep, you're definitely a lot easier on the eyes than that old hag would have been."

Christina's heart turned over as she suppressed a tiny giggle. "Oh, Seth, I really am sorry about—"

"No, I'm the one who's sorry. I've given the past way too much power over my present...and my future." He took her hand. "I'd really like to buy you that dinner now, if you think you can stand sitting across the table from me."

The first thought that popped into her mind was, *Are you kidding? You're pretty easy on the eyes, yourself, Seth Austin.* Instead, with a dignified tilt of her chin, she said, "Why, sir, I thought you'd never ask."

With Gracie between them, Seth walked Christina inside, and the very understanding hostess showed them to an out-of-the-way booth where Gracie could comfortably lie down at Christina's feet.

After they placed their orders and a basket of chips and salsa was between them, Christina had to ask. "Why, Seth? You didn't have to bring me for Mexican food just to have it out with me about what I used to do for a living."

"You're right, and I almost didn't." He pondered a misshapen tortilla chip. "But you may recall I've got this grandmother who thinks she's the boss. She said if

I backed out on our date—her word, not mine—she'd never make my favorite dessert for me again."

Christina wiggled her brows. "Wow, she drives a hard bargain."

"If you knew how much I love strawberry-rhubarb pie, you wouldn't joke." He sank a chip deep into the salsa bowl then popped it into his mouth.

"Hmm, I think I need to remember this." Taking out her notebook and pen, Christina turned to a clean page. After printing S-E-T-H across the top in large block letters, she wrote the number *one* in the margin, followed by *Bribe with strawberry-rhubarb pie*.

Seth leaned across the table. "What are you writing in there?"

Grinning, she showed him. "Just collecting ammunition in case I ever need it."

"That's just plain mean." With a feigned pout, he flicked a chip crumb at her. "And after I apologized and everything."

She liked this playful, funny side of Seth Austin. Liked it very much. She wished he'd let it out more often.

He crossed his arms. "Now what are you smiling about?"

"I was thinking what a nice guy you can be when you really try."

Long after lights-out that night, Seth lay awake replaying the day's events. He'd been so ready to cut Christina out of his life completely, and then she disarmed him, first with the line about the crotchety old hag, but most of all, with the undeniable goodness of who she was.

He was falling hard, way too hard, and it terrified him.

On Friday, with the Finches still in residence, weekend

guests arriving after lunch and another lakeside barbecue to prepare for, Seth ran himself ragged. First up were barn chores, then the Finches' daily riding lessons and trail ride. After lunch, he hauled a wagonload of table decorations down to the picnic area for Christina before checking on Opi and the meat smoker.

The tempting aroma of mesquite-smoked brisket filled the air as Seth watched his grandfather tend the meat and add more mesquite chips. "You need to teach me your secret."

Opi banged down the smoker lid. "I ain't at death's door yet, sonny-boy."

The uncharacteristic bitterness in his grandfather's tone made Seth wince. "I didn't mean anything. I'd just like to learn."

Lips pursed, Opi lowered his head. "And I'm getting too tetchy. It's all this talk about me retiring. First the doc, and now your grandmother—nag, nag, nag. I s'pose you'll be after me next."

"Nagging's not my style." Seth gave his grandfather an affectionate pinch to the back of the neck. "However, if it'll keep you alive and kicking a good while longer, I'm willing to give it a try."

"You do and I'll knock you clean into the next county." With a frustrated shake of his head, Opi sank into a plastic patio chair. "Can't help it. The idea of being put out to pasture like a washed-up ol' cow pony doesn't appeal."

"Nobody's blaming you for that." Seth pulled another chair over and slouched down next to his grandfather. Hands folded across his belt buckle, he gazed out across the hills, the only home he'd known since his dad was killed and he and his mom came to live at her parents' ranch. Then a few years later, Mom had taken up with a nice widower from church, and after they married, her new husband's company transferred them to Denver. A sophomore in high school by then, Seth had begged to stay with his grandparents in Juniper Bluff, and Mom had reluctantly agreed.

This was his life now, and he loved every minute of it. This was why he'd begged Georgia not to leave, why he'd resisted so hard following her to Minneapolis. So he understood exactly why his grandfather didn't want to let the ranch go.

And after working with the accounts yesterday, he understood even better the uphill battle they faced to keep Serenity Hills in the black.

After a few minutes, Seth rose with a tired sigh. "Guess I'd better make sure the kids aren't driving Omi up the wall while she's trying to cook."

"Or..." Opi cast him a one-eyed smirk. "You could go help your sweetie with the picnic setup."

"She's not my—" Teeth clamped together, Seth looked toward the lake. He didn't see Christina anywhere, just the utility wagon parked at an odd angle and gingham tablecloths flapping in the breeze.

His legs propelled him down the hill before he could think twice, while his gaze swept back and forth for any sign of Christina or her dog. What if she'd had another cramp, or a panic attack? What if she'd gotten so dizzy that she stumbled into the lake and drowned? A million bone-chilling scenarios bombarded his brain.

Slowing as he neared the picnic area, he called out, acutely aware of the ragged sound of his voice. "Christina! Where are you?"

"Dad!" Joseph's shout rang out from the far side of the lake. "We're over here!"

Seth spotted his son near a copse of live oaks and cedars. Heart pounding, he yelled, "What are you doing? Is Christina with you?"

"Yeah, come see! We found a baby possum."

"Don't touch it. You know better." Seth covered the distance between them and arrived out of breath, as much from release of anxiety as from the jog.

Grabbing Seth's hand, Joseph tugged him into the shade of the trees, where he found not only Christina and Gracie but Eva and the three Finch boys. They stood in a circle around a small gray creature curled up in a ball.

Seth grabbed the two nearest boys by their shoulders. "Step back, kids. Let me take a look."

Christina held firmly to Gracie's collar. "Can you tell if it's hurt?"

"Doesn't look like it." Dropping to one knee, Seth gave the possum a visual once-over, noting the animal's chest flutter with its quick breaths. "It's not a newborn, so if we leave it alone, it should be fine. Right now it's just scared." *Like I was two minutes ago.*

"You heard the man." Christina spoke with authority as she herded the children away and into the open. "You should never, ever approach a wild animal unless a grown-up is with you and knows what to do."

"Exactly." Seth sent the Finch brothers on ahead, then seized Joseph's and Eva's hands and made them face him. "What are you kids doing down here, anyway? I thought you were inside with Omi."

"Bobby asked us to come out and play," Joseph said. "Omi said it would be okay if we stayed...out of..." Mouth flattening, he glanced away.

"Stay out of trouble? With the Finch boys?" Seth rolled his eyes. "Fat chance." He should be glad his children were having fun with kids their own age for a change instead of traipsing after their dad or hanging out with their great-grandparents. But the children's newfound confidence brought a whole new set of worries, because away from Seth's or his grandparents' direct supervision, who knew what kind of dangerous situations they might fall into?

A light touch on his arm drew his attention to Christina. She looked up at him with a quirky smile. "No harm done. The kids were just being their curious selves."

Seth grimaced. "Right, a learning experience." For the kids *and* for him. He needed to get used to a whole different side of parenting. "I guess you're going to tell me I overreacted."

"It's okay, Dad." Wisdom beyond his years lit Joseph's eyes. "We know you can't help it. Anyway, we worry about you, too, sometimes."

His son's words hit him like a punch in the chest. "What?"

"Yeah, you know." Facing away from Christina, Joseph lowered his tone to a raspy whisper. "'Cause you need a girlfriend."

Seth cast a stunned look in Christina's direction. She and her dog had moved several steps away, and Seth couldn't tell whether she'd overheard Joseph's remark or not. Throat thickening, he dropped to his haunches and drew both children into his arms. "Hey, you two, the last thing you need to worry about is my, uh…dating arrangements. Besides, I've got plenty on my plate just keeping y'all out of trouble."

Eva's tiny fingers tugged on the hair at Seth's nape. "But Daddy, don't you like Miss Christina?"

"Sure I do." He forced down a swallow. Good grief,

first his grandmother, then the dog and now his kids were pushing them together? He was doomed.

Christina softly cleared her throat. "Excuse me, I'd better finish with the picnic setup."

"Wait." Seth pushed to his feet. "Kids, go on back to the house. You can ask Omi for a snack."

As the children cheered and raced up the hill, Christina folded her arms and shot Seth an uneasy smile. "One thing the accident *didn't* affect was my hearing. Believe me, I'm not reading anything into last night. I'm just happy we cleared the air and can hopefully be friends now."

The dreaded *friends* word. Seth gnawed the inside of his lip. "What if I might be ready for more?"

She looked at him like he'd just sprouted another head. "Wh-what are you saying, Seth?"

"I don't know." Pivoting a quarter-turn, he mauled the back of his head while staring across the lake, its calm surface contrasting sharply with his turbulent state of mind. "Ever since I lost Georgia, I never once felt the need to bring someone new into my life." His gaze shifted to Christina, and one corner of his mouth drifted upward in a bewildered grin. "Until you came along, anyway."

"Oh, Seth." Christina tilted her head, and Seth couldn't tell whether her smile spoke sympathy or regret.

Except now he couldn't stop looking at her. Stepping closer, he stuffed his hands deep into his jeans pockets, the only way he could resist taking her in his arms. "Yeah, I know it's crazy. But nothing's the same since you got here. Not me, not the kids. And scared as I am about all these changes, I'm liking them, too. So I'm wondering—"

Christina lifted a hand, palm outward, in a clear signal to stop. "You're my employer, Seth. It wouldn't be right. Anyway, this is a vulnerable time for you. You've shaped your whole life around your children, and now that they're separating from you a little bit, you're grappling with unfamiliar feelings. You shouldn't be rushing into any new relationships."

Seth snorted. "Don't you dare use your social-worker psychobabble on me. You think I don't know my own mind?"

"I think you just need time to sort things out." She lowered her gaze. "That's all I'm saying."

He stared at her long and hard, breaking off only when her fingers dug deep into Gracie's ruff and a nervous twitch started in her jaw muscles. He blinked and took a breath. "We've both got jobs to do. Best get after it."

As he strode past her, he thought he heard the tiniest of whimpers, but he couldn't afford to stop and offer comfort. She was a social worker, after all. Let her figure it out for herself.

Gracie's insistent whining and pressure against Christina's leg finally broke through. Striving for calm, Christina forced her breathing into a slow, deliberate rhythm.

She should have known better than to haul out the Psych 101 jargon with Seth. Worse, she didn't know what unnerved her more—Seth's interest in pursuing a relationship, or that she might actually like the idea.

Face it, you're no more ready for romance than he is. They both needed to get their lives, and their emotions, straightened out first. And by then, Christina would be on her way back to Little Rock and the fulfilling career she missed so desperately. There was no possible way Seth fit into her future.

With a final exhalation, she squared her shoulders and patted Gracie's head. "All better now, girl. Let's finish setting up for the barbecue."

She was starting to get the hang of putting those bluebonnet centerpieces together. Once all the silk flowers, greenery, candles and hurricane globes were in place, she stepped back to admire her handiwork. Next came the task of loading the plastic crates into the wagon and dragging it to the storeroom. Bracing herself for the inevitable ache in her hip, she gripped the wagon handle and started up the hill. No chance of Prince Charming coming to her rescue this time. Seth had disappeared into the barn, and she doubted she'd see him again before the evening festivities began.

The glacial crevasse she'd created between them brought a clutch to her chest. Why couldn't he leave well enough alone? Besides, there was a charming and highly motivated young woman in town who clearly would like nothing more than to snag Seth's affections. The unwelcome memory of Diana Matthews's overt flirting at the chili cook-off made Christina's stomach clench with an emotion she refused to acknowledge as jealousy.

Envy, maybe, because she longed for the freedom and self-confidence to live life on her own terms again. And Diana certainly exuded self-confidence. She'd make a great mom and role model for Seth's kids. He should wake up and smell the coffee, a big ol' mug of it at Diana's Donuts.

After parking the utility wagon in the storeroom, Christina was ready to relax in her cabin with a cold drink. As she exited the storeroom, an unfamiliar rumble drew her up short. Mouth falling open, she stared at Gracie. "Are you *growling* at me?"

If dogs could glare, Gracie was doing just that. The growl deepened, not really a menacing sound, but apparently the dog had begun to take her job a tad too seriously.

Hands on hips, Christina shook her head. "I don't know what's got into you lately, girl, but it has to stop."

"Problems?"

She looked up to see Marie coming her way. "I think Gracie may need some retraining."

Tail wagging, Gracie spun around and trotted over to greet Marie, who bent to fondle the dog's ears.

Christina harrumphed. "See what I mean? She doesn't even remember when she's supposed to be on duty anymore."

"My fault." Marie offered an apologetic smile. "I should know better than to pet her without your permission."

"No, it's okay." Heaving a sigh, Christina tightened her ponytail. "Did you need me to do something else before I take a short break?"

"Actually, I was about to invite you inside for some raspberry iced tea and cookies—and a chat," Marie added with a meaningful lift of one brow. "I was hoping you'd be a little more forthcoming than Seth about how last night went—*and* what's going on with you two today."

Christina's stomach twisted. She really didn't want to get into a discussion with Marie about where things stood with Seth. Mainly because she wasn't so sure herself. It would be awfully hard to continue working here if they couldn't come to a comfortable understanding.

She toed a clump of grass at the edge of the path. "The tea sounds great, but I don't know what I could add to what Seth already told you."

"Are you kidding? Anything you tell me will be

more than I'm getting from him." Marie hooked her arm through Christina's. "Let's go, young lady, because my curiosity is not to be denied."

Naturally, Gracie already trotted ahead of them toward the porch, tongue lolling and tail wagging as if she'd known the plan all along. *Smarty-pants*.

In the kitchen, Marie filled two tall tumblers with crushed ice from the fridge dispenser, then poured fresh-brewed tea rich with the sweet scent of raspberries. After handing the glasses to Christina, she carried a cellophane-covered plate of oatmeal-raisin cookies to the trestle table. They sat down kitty-cornered from each other.

Peeling aside the cellophane, Marie laid a cookie on a napkin and passed it to Christina. "First of all, I'm real sorry for the way Seth found out you're a social worker. He doesn't usually spend much time in the office, so I never expected he'd go snooping through the files."

Christina gave a tired shrug as she broke off a small bite from the cookie. "He was bound to find out sooner or later."

"Once he told me what happened, I *made* him keep his date with you. Figured if y'all hashed it out face-to-face, he'd realize what a pigheaded horse's rear he was being."

Christina stifled a chuckle at Marie's unlikely metaphor. "He mentioned your threat of no more strawberry-rhubarb pie."

"I know how to fight dirty when I have to." Marie traced a line of condensation on her iced tea glass. "So what's up with y'all today? Seth was in a mighty good mood this morning, but last time I saw him, he was spitting nails. Gave me all kinds of what-for because I let the kids go out and play."

"He was scared, that's all." Christina liked and respected Marie too much to shift back into social-worker mode. This conversation called for friend-to-friend honesty. "And I...I think I hurt his feelings."

"Now, *that* makes more sense." Marie cast a furtive glance toward the hallway. "What I told you yesterday, well, it sure would put my mind at ease to know Seth was moving on with his life, too. For his sake and for the kids. They're getting attached to you, Christina. All of them. And I'm praying... I'm just praying you'll give Seth a chance."

Christina sucked in a tiny gasp. "Oh, Marie, you don't know what you're asking."

"Oh, but I do, sweet girl." A wistful smile turned up one corner of her mouth. "I first laid eyes on Bryan when he beat the record-holder's time bustin' a bronc at the county rodeo. My girlfriend and I had both ridden in the Grand Entry that afternoon, and after Bryan won his event, all the pretty cowgirls were crowding around asking for his autograph. I was a shy one back then, but my girlfriend dragged me to the front of the line. When I handed Bryan my program, he looked straight into my eyes and smiled like I was the only one there, and that's when he stole my heart. We started dating, then got married exactly three months later, and I've never had a moment's regret."

"I'm happy for you," Christina murmured, her throat tight with emotion. She gave Marie's hand a squeeze. "But my situation is different. I've got—"

"Baggage. I know. And so does Seth. But when it comes to emptying suitcases, the job goes a lot faster and easier if you have help." Marie's gaze became pleading. "You two could be so good for each other. And those kids—why, honey, you've got them wrapped around your little finger. If you'd only—"

The back door opened, and Seth strode in, boots clomping on the tile floor. He stopped at the end of the bar, his glance flitting between Christina and his grandmother. "Where are the kids?" he asked gruffly.

Marie dashed her hand across a damp cheek. "Joseph's playing one of his video games. I put Eva down for a nap."

"Good, it'll be a late night." Seth's jaw worked as if he couldn't decide whether to go or stay.

With a rough clear of her throat, Marie stood. "You look hot. Take my seat, and I'll pour you a glass of tea."

Christina decided this might be a good time to excuse herself, but Seth pinned her to the spot with his sharp stare. He didn't speak, and he made no move to sit down.

The fridge dispenser groaned as Marie filled two more glasses with crushed ice. She poured tea, then handed one of the glasses to Seth. "I'm taking the other one out to your grandpa."

"Let me—"

"I said sit," she commanded in the bossy tone Christina was growing all too familiar with. "And keep an eye out the front window. The weekend guests should be driving up anytime now."

Christina held herself rigid as Seth lowered himself stiffly into the chair Marie had vacated. Maybe if she waited until Marie stepped outside, she could make her escape. She started to reach for Gracie, but the dog chose that moment to get up from her spot next to Christina's chair and meander across the room. With a gaping yawn, Gracie stretched out in front of the back door. If Christina tried to leave now, she'd have to get her dog to move, and the way Gracie had been acting lately, cooperation didn't appear likely.

Seth's tea glass hit the table with a *thunk*, and Christina flinched. "You realize we've been set up again," he said.

Christina glared at her traitorous dog. "I think Gracie and your grandmother are in cahoots."

"Wouldn't surprise me." Stretching out one leg, Seth heaved a sigh. "I'm sorry for losing my cool earlier. I made assumptions I shouldn't have."

"I'm sorry, too. I said I wanted to be friends, and friends don't psychoanalyze each other."

Seth's mouth twitched ominously. "Yeah, about the *friends* thing…"

"We've been through this already. Please, Seth—"

He held up one hand. "Just hear me out, okay? I get all the reasons you want to keep this platonic, and if I was thinking straight, I'd cut my losses and drop the whole thing." Sitting forward, he inched his hand across the table toward Christina. "But I haven't been thinking straight since the day I stopped you in the middle of the road so I could move that turtle out of the way."

Fingers itching to bury themselves in Gracie's fur, Christina knotted her fists in her lap. "That's exactly why we shouldn't be having this conversation—because neither of us is thinking straight right now."

"Then you feel it, too." Seth's gaze sharpened. "Don't deny it, Christina. You know there's something happening between us. Why can't you at least give it a chance?"

"Because—" Closing her eyes briefly, she swallowed hard. "Because I'm scared."

Seth scooted his chair closer and covered Christina's hands with his own. Looking deeply into her eyes, he said, "Then don't you think it's time we both faced our fears? Whatever the future holds for us, individually or together, I know I'll be a better person for having you in my life."

Every ounce of logic within her argued against the wisdom of saying yes. But another voice spoke louder: *You know you want this. And you know Seth is right. It's time to confront your fears—all of them—and see where life takes you.*

A teardrop slipped down her cheek and plopped onto the back of Seth's hand. Freeing one of her thumbs, she massaged away the wetness, then dug deep for the courage to meet his gaze. "Okay," she murmured, then hiked her chin higher. "Okay. As long as we agree to take things one day at a time."

Chapter Ten

If six-foot-two cowboys could float on air, that pretty much described how Seth made it through the weekend. When the next round of ranch guests checked in late Friday afternoon, they probably wondered why he couldn't keep a stupid grin off his face.

He wondered, too, because he hadn't felt this giddy over a girl since he was a teenager. During a quiet moment in the barn on Monday while he groomed Tango for a training ride, it occurred to him that not even Georgia had discombobulated him so thoroughly.

Tango must have picked up on his jitters, too, acting more skittish than usual as he saddled her up. Out in the arena, she overreacted to every little squeeze of his legs or pressure on the reins. He finally gave up, deciding to postpone their practice session until his state of mind had leveled out.

His grandfather met him in the barn, the kids tagging along. "Quitting already?"

"Seems we're both having an off day." Seth secured Tango in the cross-ties and loosened the saddle cinch.

"Guess that makes four of us."

Seth's brow furrowed. "Four?"

"You and Tango, plus myself, for reasons you are well aware of." Opi nodded toward Joseph. "And this little guy's got something on his mind, too."

"Oh, yeah?" After dropping Tango's tack onto a wooden saddle stand, Seth knelt in front of his son. "What's up, kiddo?"

Thumbs tucked in his jeans pockets, Joseph heaved an exaggerated sigh. "Do we *have* to do homeschool again?"

"Well, yeah, son. You have to keep up your studies."

"That's not what I mean." Joseph glanced up at Opi, who offered an encouraging smile. "Daddy, I want to go to the real school. With my friends."

Seth nearly choked on his surprised gasp. "Wow."

"So can I? It starts in two days, and I'd be in the same class as Darin and Hayden from Sunday school."

"Public school would be a really big step for you." *And for me.* Seth looked deep into his son's eyes. "Are you sure you're ready?"

"I'm a big kid now. I'm almost ten years old."

"That you are." Standing upright, Seth rubbed his jaw. "In that case, we'd better head over to the school and get you registered."

A tug on his pants leg drew his attention to Eva. She cupped one hand around her mouth and whispered, "You can still be my teacher, Daddy. I don't want to go to the big school."

"That's just fine, sweetie." Seth tousled her mop of blond curls. "There's no rush."

"Can we go right now, Dad?" Joseph begged. "And then go buy school supplies and clothes and stuff?"

"Hold your horses, boy!" Laughing, Seth waved both hands in the air. "You kinda sprung this on me, so give me a minute or two to get my head around the idea. How about we plan on going right after lunch?"

"Yes!" Joseph pumped a fist. "And can Miss Christina go with us? I want to show her my new school."

At the mention of Christina's name, Seth's heart flipped. "Sure, I'll ask if she wants to go along."

Opi shot Seth a knowing wink. "Come on, kids, we've got tack to clean after last weekend, and I'm counting on your help."

While his grandfather took the children into the tack room, Seth brushed the sweat marks on Tango's back, then led the mare out to her pasture. With a spring in his step, he went looking for Christina—not hard since he quickly spotted Gracie napping on the cabin four porch. Christina must be inside cleaning.

Striding up to the open door, Seth stepped around Gracie and peeked inside. Swishing sounds came from the bathroom, along with the strong scent of disinfectant cleaner. Cleaning up after the Finch boys—a wave of sympathy for Christina swept over him. He tapped on the door frame and called her name.

"Oh, hi, Seth." Blowing a limp strand off her forehead, she appeared with a load of wet towels. "I had no idea any human being could get so creative with toothpaste. I think there's even some on the ceiling, but you might have to reach it for me."

"Glad to." He grabbed a cleaning rag and headed into the bathroom. "Man, I'm sorry you got stuck doing this. The housekeeper we had last year nearly quit the first time she had to clean after the Finches."

"Wimp."

Seth swiped at a greenish blob next to the ceiling light. Yep, toothpaste. If the Finches came back next year, the ranch might need to require a security deposit. He checked around for other spots, then tossed the soiled cloth onto the cart.

Christina had started stripping beds, and Seth joined in to help. He shook out a pillowcase. "How much do you have left to do?"

"This one and I'm done. I saved the worst for last." She gathered up an armful of sheets and dropped them by the door. "I know the ranch needs the business, but I won't complain about a few days off before the next round of guests."

"Me neither." He sidled up next to Christina as she counted out a fresh set of fluffy white towels. Purposely invading her space, he reached around her for a stack of sheets.

She shot him a mock scowl and bumped him aside with her hip. "Don't you have something else you should be doing? Like maybe filling that bear trap Bobby Finch dug on the other side of the lake?"

"Hmm, might need to catch a bear one of these days." It had been way too long since the last time Seth enjoyed casual banter with a pretty girl. Sure, he sometimes joked with Diana when he stopped in the doughnut shop, and there was the redhead checkout girl at the supermarket who liked to flirt.

But this was different. This was…special. And it made Seth *feel* special. With Christina he was more than an old high school chum or a likely target for a single woman looking for Mr. Right. He was more than an overworked ranch manager, more than Joseph and Eva's dad. When Christina looked at him, he felt hopeful. He felt whole.

He felt like a man.

"Those sheets don't unfold themselves, you know."

Blinking several times, he stared at the forgotten stack of linens in his hands. Christina was already halfway upstairs to the loft with three more sets of sheets. While listening to her rustle around overhead, he went to work on the queen-size bed and hoped he remembered how to make hospital corners. He wasn't nearly as particular about his own room.

Christina finished long before he did and pitched in to help him complete the job. While she gathered up her cleaning supplies, he shoved all the dirty laundry into the canvas bag attached to the maid's cart.

"Allow me." With a crisp bow, Seth pushed the cart through the door. When Gracie scurried out of the way, he said, "Sorry, girl. Nap time's over."

Ambling along beside him, Christina cast him a whimsical grin. "What would I do without my knight in shining armor to rescue me from this toil and strain?"

He wanted to say, *I hope you never have to find out.* But they weren't to that stage of their relationship, at least not yet, and he didn't want to scare her off. "Think you might be rested up enough this afternoon to go into town with Joseph and me?"

"Possibly. Why?"

Seth told her what Joseph had asked him in the barn earlier.

Mouth falling open, she jerked to a halt. "He wants to enroll in public school? That's awesome!"

Stopping a few steps ahead, Seth turned to face her, his own disbelief still sharp. "It's all because of you, you know."

"Oh, Seth, no." Closing the gap between them, Christina held out her hands to him, and he took them gladly. "Even in the short time I've known Joseph, I could tell he'd be coming into his own soon. He's smart and fun and such a wonderful big brother to Eva."

Drawing her closer, he encircled her waist with his arms. "So…you think he would have done okay in spite of having a severely overprotective dad?"

"You'd be surprised how resilient kids are."

Seth arched a brow. "Is that Christina talking, or Ms. Hunter the social worker?"

In a tiny voice, she answered, "Will I get in trouble if I say both?"

"I'm through dissing social workers—well, maybe except for one who shall remain nameless." Oh, man, how he wanted to kiss this woman! With a ragged sigh, he released her and locked his fingers firmly around the cart handle. "We'd better finish up so we can grab lunch and get to town."

"Yes, right." Did she sound as flustered as he felt just now?

As Christina marched up the hill ahead of him, Seth reminded himself again that she couldn't be rushed. And for the sake of his own heart, he needed to take things slowly. The deepest part of him reached heavenward to the God he'd mostly been ignoring the last few years.

Lord, I never knew how much I needed Christina until she came into my life. If this is meant to be, it's all on You.

Christina felt honored to be invited along to register Joseph for school. Once Seth had filled out all the paperwork and the principal had given them a tour, they headed up the highway to a discount department store. Christina helped Joseph pick out new shirts, jeans and sneakers. Then they checked off items on his school supplies list, including an insulated lunchbox and a fancy gray backpack with silver racing stripes.

It was nearing five o'clock by the time they returned to the ranch, and Christina sighed with a different kind of fatigue.

"You okay?" Seth asked as he helped her get Gracie down from the pickup. Joseph had already made a beeline for the house to show off his new school things.

"Just thinking what a great afternoon we had. Wasn't it fun to see Joseph's eyes light up when he saw his classroom?"

"Yeah, that was cool." He shut the door and rested one shoulder against it, standing so close that Christina could almost count the threads in his shirt collar. "Thanks for going along. It meant a lot to Joseph…and to me."

How many times in the last few days had she sensed he was about to kiss her?

How many times had she wished he would?

He took her hand, lightly drawing his thumb across her knuckles and sending shivers up her spine. "Have supper with us tonight. You know Omi always cooks plenty."

She breathed in the faint citrusy aroma of his aftershave. "Thanks, but I left some ground turkey thawing in my fridge."

"Won't it keep till tomorrow?" His fingers wove through hers, and his tone grew husky. "Today was really special. I don't want it to be over yet."

Gracie nosed between them, a plea in her limpid brown eyes.

Christina laughed. "This time, Seth, I think we're both outvoted. Somebody wants her own supper." With a gentle tug, she freed her hand. "Anyway, I really am tired." And not just physically. As enjoyable as the afternoon had been, it had drained her emotionally, as well. More than once, she found herself caught up in the fantasy of Seth and his children as her family. It had all seemed so normal—taking their little boy to see his new school, shopping for supplies, stopping for ice-cream cones on the way home—as if they really were a comfortable old married couple.

Seth gave Gracie's head a scratch. "Wouldn't want this girl to go hungry." He smiled, but his voice carried a tinge of disappointment. "See you tomorrow?"

"You know where to find me."

By the time Christina stepped through her cabin door, the turkey tacos she'd planned for her supper didn't sound nearly as appealing as they had when she'd picked up the ingredients at the supermarket the other day.

No, if she were honest, what didn't appeal was the idea of eating them *alone.*

"Nothing against you, girl," she said as Gracie slurped mouthfuls of kibble. "But your dinner conversation skills are severely lacking."

With chopped onions, garlic and ground turkey simmering on the stove, Christina diced a tomato and shredded some lettuce. She wrapped two flour tortillas in a damp paper towel and laid them in the microwave, ready to heat up as soon as the meat mixture was ready.

Feeling a headache coming on, she sank into one of the dinette chairs and rested her head on her folded arms.

The next thing she knew, Gracie was whining and anxiously nudging her side. Catching the acrid smell of burnt turkey, Christina sprinted to the stove and turned off the gas burner. "Thank you, girl!"

After examining the remains of the taco filling, Christina decided enough was salvageable that she wouldn't go hungry. While the tortillas warmed, she filled a water glass and set out a plate. A few minutes later, she dined on soft tacos with a definite charred flavor.

Climbing into bed later, she let her thoughts drift back over the day's events...and the look in Seth's eyes as they'd parted earlier. Oh, she was in dangerous territory now. If she grew any more attached to this man and his kids, how could she ever bear to leave when the time came? And she knew it must, because she could not let herself relinquish hope of returning to the career she loved. The whole point of taking this job was to reclaim her independence, to prove to herself and her family that she was not an invalid in need of special treatment.

Instinctively, she reached for the dog curled up beside her, fingers entwining the soft fur behind Gracie's ears.

Gracie. Her service dog. A reminder that Christina wasn't yet whole. If Gracie hadn't roused her when supper started burning, the whole cabin might have gone up in flames, and Christina with it.

The dog shifted slightly and licked the tip of Christina's nose.

"I know, puppy-girl. I love you, too."

The next few days were easy in some ways, harder in others. With summer vacation coming to a close, cabin reservations slacked off even more, which meant Christina's housekeeping chores would be minimal until Friday, when a couple of weekend guests were due to arrive.

The hard part was staying busy enough to keep a comfortable distance between her and Seth, because with each passing day he seemed more intent on spending time with her. On Tuesday he invited her along on a horseback ride with him and the kids, but she declined, saying she had some personal things to catch up on.

The next day, when Seth found out she planned a trip into town to pick up groceries, he offered to drive her. Without a good excuse to turn him down, she accepted. Then she spent the entire thirty-two minutes in the supermarket (yes, she counted every minute) pretending not to notice the curious looks and approving nods Seth earned from acquaintances he ran into—and in a small town like Juniper Bluff, there were plenty.

But it was nice, because in the short time Christina had known Seth, she hadn't seen him smile this much or appear so at ease in his own skin. He even seemed more relaxed with the kids, his overprotectiveness subsiding to more normal levels appropriate for an attentive, caring parent. And clearly the changes in Seth were having an effect on Joseph and Eva. Joseph's excitement about attending public school with his friends was a huge step in itself, but both the children seemed less clingy overall. More than once, Christina had to resist the urge to skewer Seth with a friendly "I told you so."

On Sunday morning, while the guests were at breakfast, Seth found her tidying one of the cabins. Leaning in the open door, he folded his arms and offered a shy grin. "I'll be taking the kids to Sunday school and church in a bit. Think you could break away and join us?"

She tried to keep the surprise out of her tone. "Your grandparents aren't attending today?"

"Once a month there's a Sunday evening prayer service. They're going after the guests check out."

"That sounds nice." Turning away, Christina set fresh cups next to the in-room coffeemaker. "I should probably wait and go with them. I still have another cabin to do."

Seth handed her two cellophane-wrapped coffee service packets. "I'll help. We don't have to leave for another half hour." His voice fell to a murmur. "Please, Christina, come with me. It's been awhile since I've had much interest in going to church, but this morning I feel like it's where I need to be."

The quiet plea in his tone got her attention. Heart softening, she swiveled to face him. "In that case, I'd love to go with you."

Together they made quick work of the remaining cabin, then Seth put the cleaning cart and supplies away while Christina hurried to her own cabin to freshen up. With Gracie at her side, she met him at his pickup a few minutes later.

"Yay, Miss Christina's coming with Gracie!" Eva wrapped one arm around Gracie's neck and the other around Christina's legs. "Can Gracie come to my Sunday school class again?"

Christina tugged on one of Eva's curls. "How about we walk you to your class and see how it goes? Because today might be the day you feel brave enough to go in all by yourself."

Looking up at her dad, Eva cast him a doubtful frown. "You could go with me then, Daddy."

"Like Miss Christina said, we'll see how it goes, okay?" Seth lifted his daughter into the back seat and buckled her in.

On the drive into town, Joseph used his big-brother logic plus plenty of braggadocio after a successful first three days in public school to try to convince Eva she could go to class on her own. She wasn't buying it, though, and sat with her arms crossed and glaring out the side window. When Seth finally told Joseph to cool it, his tone gentle but as firm as Christina had ever heard him use on his kids, she had to look out her own window and cover her mouth to stifle a chuckle.

Seth gave her a friendly punch on the arm. "What are you laughing at?"

Her grin widened. "I'm afraid to tell you or you'll hit me again."

"And you'd probably deserve it." He grinned back, and the warmth of his gaze ignited feelings Christina had been trying hard to ignore for the past week.

At church, they walked Joseph to his Sunday school class, then continued on to Eva's. Her teacher met them at the door and knelt to greet Eva with a cheery smile. "I see you brought your friends again," the woman said with a nod toward Christina and Gracie. "Will they be joining you today?"

Eva glanced up at her dad, then at Christina. The indecision in her little face made Christina's chest constrict.

"I have an idea." Christina gave Eva's shoulder an encouraging squeeze. "What if you go on in with your teacher while Gracie and your dad and I stay right here by the door. We won't leave until you're all settled and your teacher begins the lesson."

"Great idea," the teacher said. Without giving Eva too much time to think about it, she took her by the hand and led her to a seat.

When the girl in the next chair greeted Eva with a happy hello, she seemed to forget all about being scared.

Taking Christina's hand, Seth drew her to the opposite side of the corridor. "See what I mean? You've been so good for my kids." His voice grew husky. "And for me."

She glanced around uncomfortably—they were at church, after all. This was worse than at the supermarket the other day. "Shouldn't we get to the adult Bible study? It's almost time to start."

With a nervous brush of his nape, Seth peered over his shoulder toward the adult classroom. He looked almost as uncertain as Eva had moments ago.

"It'll be all right," Christina said in her most kid-friendly tone. "Gracie and I will go in with you, and if you get too scared, you can hug my dog."

Seth released an embarrassed laugh. "Thanks, I think that'll help a lot."

When he rested his palm at Christina's waist to escort her into the classroom, she hoped no one would notice the blush heating her cheeks. They took chairs at the end of the back row, where Gracie could lie on the floor next to Christina. With Seth cradling her left hand on his thigh, she soon found herself reaching for Gracie with her other hand.

And silently praying, because if Seth Austin worked his way any deeper into her affections, not even her faithful service dog could protect her fragile heart.

Chapter Eleven

Six weeks. That's how long since the first time Seth had laid eyes on Christina Hunter. It seemed like only yesterday…and as if he'd been waiting for her all his life.

Sure, they still had a lot to learn about each other, but at least she wasn't holding back like she had at first. They'd been to church together twice now, taken the kids on a couple of trail rides, and last night they'd shared a sunset picnic by the lake, courtesy of Omi's kitchen talents and Opi's guitar serenade. Thankfully, Opi had the good sense to quietly take his leave at an opportune moment, leaving Seth and Christina alone to watch the stars popping out.

And he'd kissed her. Just a quick one, nothing über-romantic and barely skimming her lips. He'd have liked it to be more, but in this getting-to-know-you phase, he still counted it as progress.

"Seth. Seth!" Omi's demanding tone broke into his thoughts. "Have you heard a single thing I've said?"

Blinking rapidly, he poked his fork into a slice of breakfast sausage. "Sorry, still half-asleep."

"Or mooning over your sweetie again." She snorted

and refilled his coffee mug. "We need to talk about some stuff. Join me in the office after you get back from taking Joseph to school."

The seriousness of her tone made his gut clench. "What's wrong? Is it Opi's heart again?"

She shot a quick glance toward the hallway. "No, but it might be if he keeps fretting over finances. Like I said, you and I need to talk."

Seth nodded. After washing down the last few bites of eggs and sausage with a long swig of coffee, he went upstairs to hurry Joseph along. The twice-a-day trip to town took a sizable chunk out of Seth's schedule, but even though a school bus passed right by the ranch turnoff, Seth still felt protective enough that he needed to personally deliver his son to and from the school building each day.

When he returned from the morning school run, he glimpsed Opi leading one of the horses out to pasture, Eva happily trotting along on her stick horse beside him. Maybe they'd stay outside while Seth's grandmother shared whatever was on her mind.

Seth found her working at the office computer, her expression grim. He plopped down in one of the barrel chairs. "That bad, huh?"

"You don't know the half of it." With a tired shake of her head, she swiveled to face him. "Either people aren't spending as much on vacations this year or they're opting for fancier destinations than a no-frills guest ranch like ours."

"We've kept it simple on purpose. If folks want high-speed internet, cable TV in every room and a heated swimming pool, they can have their pick of hotel chains." Seth massaged his jaw. "Maybe we need to advertise more. Or put up the website we've never gotten around to doing."

"I'm afraid it'd all be too little, too late." Omi eyed a brochure on the corner of the desk as if it were a scorpion about to strike. "The Carsons up the road just decided to sell out to a developer who's gonna subdivide their land into four-acre ranchettes, put in a clubhouse, pool, riding trails, nine-hole golf course, the works. If we could interest him in our property—"

"No way!" Seth slammed the desk with his open palm. "I don't care how bad off we are, nobody's going to slice and dice Serenity Hills."

"It's not what I want either, son. But this place was supposed to be yours someday. An inheritance for you and those precious kids. At this rate, it's only going to leave you in deeper and deeper debt."

Sausage and eggs churned in Seth's stomach. "Does Opi know about the Carsons?"

"Not yet. I only found out when I ran into Harriet at the drugstore yesterday and she gave me this brochure." Omi speared Seth with a sharp stare. "And don't you dare say a word to your grandpa. It'll send his blood pressure through the roof."

"He'll find out sooner or later." Seth glared right back. "Anyway, weren't you just trying to convince me that selling was a good idea?"

With a weary sigh, Omi rested her head in her hands. "All I know is, things can't continue as they are. If I don't get your grandpa off the ranch, he'll either work himself to death or worry himself to death, and neither option's okay with me."

Seth circled the desk and wrapped his grandmother in a hug. "We'll figure something out, okay? I promise."

A promise he had no idea yet how he'd keep. With a kiss to the top of Omi's head, Seth slipped out. He had some serious thinking to do, and he did his best thinking on the back of a horse.

As he headed out to Tango's pasture, he glimpsed Opi and Eva strolling down to the lake with fishing gear. It gave his heart a turn to see his grandfather looking happy and relaxed, whistling a jaunty tune while Eva darted to and fro inspecting blades of grass and wildflowers. *This* was Serenity Hills, the way it was always meant to be, and Seth couldn't bear the thought of things changing.

But he wasn't oblivious, either. He'd spent enough time examining the ranch accounts recently to know his grandmother hadn't exaggerated the seriousness of their situation. He'd already put up notices at the feed store advertising the trail horses he hoped to sell. Buckling Tango's halter, he swallowed over the lump in his throat. Worth more than all their herd put together, Tango was the horse he ought to be offering for sale. His dreams of breeding show horses were just that—dreams.

Teeth clenched, he tugged out his cell phone, backed up a few steps and snapped Tango's photo from several angles. He'd upload them to several quarter horse message boards, along with her pedigree and a detailed description. Then he'd test the waters with a hefty asking price. If he found a buyer right away, he'd know it was meant to be. If not…he'd figure out his next step when the time came.

Another stretch of days without ranch guests. Christina wondered how the Petersons could continue paying her a salary, much less keep Serenity Hills afloat.

But she did love it here. And last evening with Seth under the stars…perfection. When his lips feathered hers, she secretly wished for more but was grateful he hadn't claimed what she wasn't quite ready to give. These blossoming feelings were still so new, so overwhelming, that sometimes she thought her heart would burst right out of her chest.

She hadn't even told her mother yet about this new development, and considering how hard Mom tried to wheedle information from her during their phone conversations, Christina felt pretty proud of herself for playing it cool.

Once she'd completed her minimal housekeeping duties for the day, she poured the remains of her breakfast coffee into the blender, added milk, sweetener and several ice cubes, and whipped up a frothy iced latte. She transferred the concoction to a lidded tumbler, then headed out the door with Gracie for a walk.

Seeing Seth coming her way, she started to call out. But something seemed off. Head down, shoulders stiff, he strode purposefully toward the house. On a quiet day like this, she'd normally expect to see him riding Tango in the arena. Had something happened to one of the children?

He walked right past her without even looking up, and now her mouth had gone so dry with concern that she couldn't push his name past her lips. Before she could get her feet moving to follow, he'd vanished through the back door.

Then her cell phone rang. Startled, she set her drink down and fumbled for the phone in her shorts pocket. When she read the caller's name, her stomach swooped. "Lindsey? Hi, how are you?"

"I'm great, Christina." Her former supervisor's familiar voice zinged her back through time. "Well, not *great* exactly. Which is why I'm calling."

"Why? What's wrong?"

"We need you back. Desperately."

Lindsey's plea ignited both longing and panic. One hand on Gracie's neck, Christina made her way to a circle of Adirondack chairs beneath a spreading oak tree. "I don't know what to say, Lindsey." She sank into the nearest chair. "I'd like nothing more than to come back to work, but…"

"I know you've needed time to recover, but your mom says you're doing so much better."

"I am." As Christina's gaze swept the ranch house, the barn and pastures, the lakeside picnic area, her pulse and breathing slowed. "Honestly, coming to Juniper Bluff has been the best therapy I could ask for."

"Then you're ready to get back to work, right? We're short-staffed right now, and you're one of the best, most qualified social workers I know."

"Wow. I'm honored, truly." Christina scooted sideways to avoid the doggy breath puffing across her face. "Down, girl."

"What?"

"I was talking to Gracie. She's getting almost as overprotective as my parents." Now the dog laid a paw on Christina's knee. She covered the mouthpiece and whispered, "What's going on with you, girl? Can't I even talk on the phone anymore without you butting in?"

Returning the phone to her ear, she said, "I really need to think about this, Lindsey. For one thing, I made a commitment to my employers here, and I respect them too much to leave before they can find a replacement."

"Understandable." Lindsey released a sighing breath. "But don't take too long, okay? If I know you're coming back soon, I can survive."

Ending the call, Christina leaned her head back and gazed up through the oak branches toward a crystal-blue sky. *Lord, You know I want this. Help me know if I'm ready.*

Stillness was her only answer.

Except for the pesky dog nudging her arm with a cold, wet nose.

Christina wiped her arm on her shirttail. "I love you, sweet girl, but this is getting ridiculous."

A shadow fell across her lap. "What's ridiculous?"

She jerked her head up to see Seth standing over her. "Oh, just Gracie being Gracie. I was trying to talk on the phone and—" guilt tightened her throat "—she wouldn't leave me alone."

Seth gave the dog a scratch behind the ears, then sank onto one of the other chairs. "Your mom call again?"

"No, it was…a friend." Christina shifted for a better look at Seth. "I saw you go inside earlier. You looked upset."

The furrow between his brows deepened. "Just ranch business. Nothing you need to worry about."

"But I do worry. And I feel horrible for taking a paycheck when the cabins aren't occupied."

"That's not your problem." He reached for her hand, but his smile looked forced. "We're paying you by the week, not the number of guests who check in."

She ran her thumb across his knuckles, feeling every ridge and admiring the strength in those hands, the strength in this man. Leaving him wouldn't be easy, but perhaps a clean break would be better for both of them, and for his children, too. "Seth…the call this morning… it was my supervisor from Child Protective Services."

His fingers tensed. "You mean your *former* supervisor. From before your accident."

"She wanted to know if I'm ready to come back." Christina watched Seth's face, trying to gauge his reaction. "She says they need me."

Withdrawing his hand, he nodded slowly, his gaze riveted to something on the horizon. "You've made no secret that was your plan. How soon will you go?"

His cool response made her heart twist. "Nothing's decided yet. Anyway, I wouldn't think of leaving until you find someone to replace me."

"*Replace* you?" Seth's head swung around so fast that she flinched. He gave a harsh laugh. "Sure, no prob. We'll start advertising right away." Shoving to his feet, he marched toward the house.

"Wait, Seth! You don't—"

He silenced her with a flick of his hand and kept walking.

Gracie whined and pushed her snout under Christina's arm. Only then did she notice her own shallow breathing and the rapid thump of her pulse. Burying her face in Gracie's fur, she inhaled long and slow in a desperate attempt for control.

Only this didn't feel like the typical panic attack she'd dealt with so often since the accident. This felt like loss, like being forced to choose between something she wanted desperately and someone who'd come to mean more to her than she'd ever planned on or imagined possible.

Eva latched on to Seth's leg the minute he stepped into the kitchen. "Daddy, will you play with me?"

He scooped her into his arms and kissed her temple.

Nothing like holding his little girl to take his mind off all his other problems. "What is it, sweetie? Missing Joseph?"

"I don't want him to go to the real school anymore. Why can't you and Omi teach him again?"

"Joseph likes going to school with his friends." Seth tapped the end of her nose. "Just like you will someday when you get bigger."

Eva gave her head a firm shake. "No. I'm always, always, always going to stay home with you."

Good to know somebody still wanted to keep him close. His throat shifted at the memory of what Christina had laid on him a few minutes ago. He also knew he wasn't being fair. Christina, Joseph, Eva—they each deserved the chance to discover their inner strength and find their own way in the world, and he wouldn't be the one to hold them back.

Not like he'd tried to do with Georgia.

"So will you play with me, Daddy?" Eva tugged on his shirt collar. "Omi got me a new puzzle and I need you to help me make the picture."

"Sure, hon. Let's do it." He hefted her a little higher on his hip and strode to the family room, where Eva had left puzzle pieces scattered across the coffee table.

Omi looked up from her Bible and journal. "Thought you were working Tango."

"Other things to do." Ignoring his grandmother's doubtful frown, Seth plopped onto the sofa and picked up a couple of puzzle pieces. "Look here, Eva, I think this is the princess's crown."

Omi cleared her throat meaningfully. "You aren't about to do something stupid, are you?"

"What, this isn't a princess crown?" Seth pretended to examine the piece.

"You know good and well that's not what I'm talking about." Leaning toward him, Omi lowered her voice. "I know you too well, young man. You can be mighty stubborn when you set your mind on something."

Eva held up a puzzle piece with a red corner. "Is this part of the castle flag, Daddy?"

"Could be. See if it fits."

It did, and when Eva pumped a fist the way she'd seen Joseph do, Seth chuckled and gave her a high five.

"You're doing great, honey. You keep working on it while I talk to Omi for a minute." Seth slid to the end of the sofa nearest his grandmother's chair. "Where's Opi?"

"Came in from fishing and said he needed to pick up something in town. I gave him the grocery list, so he'll be awhile." Omi set her Bible and journal aside. "Might as well spill it, 'cause you know I won't stop pestering you till you do."

Seth chewed the inside of his lip. Should he start with his intention to sell Tango, or let his grandmother know Christina was about to quit? Omi wasn't going to be happy in either case. It took him less than a second to decide Christina should be the one to give notice if and when she was ready.

As for selling Tango, Seth's grandparents would find out soon enough when potential buyers started inquiring. Checking briefly on Eva's progress, he leaned closer to his grandmother to confess what he'd decided. "And don't try to talk me out of it. I've already put the word out online."

"Seth Austin, you insufferable fool!" Omi spat the

words. "That horse is your pride and joy. You can't do this, honey. You just can't!"

Before Seth could reply, Eva worked her way beneath his arm and peered up at him with a worried frown. "Daddy, why is Omi so mad at you?"

"Aw, honey, I'm not mad." Omi stroked Eva's cheek. "It's just grown-up stuff we gotta work out between us."

"That's right, honey." Giving his daughter a reassuring hug, Seth directed her back to the puzzle. With Eva's attention diverted, he shot his grandmother a stern glance. "Actually, there's nothing more to say on the subject. So let's drop it."

She didn't look like she intended to leave it alone for long, though, and Seth knew he'd eventually have to deal with both her reaction and Opi's. In the meantime, all he wanted was to spend this time with his little girl and try to get his mind off the bombshells he'd been hit with this morning.

Why, God, why? Things had been going so well, his life on a path toward the healing he'd all but given up hope for. Now he was on the verge of losing both the home he loved and the woman he cherished more every day.

His grandmother quietly rose from her chair. As she passed by the coffee table, she laid her open Bible on the corner, then continued out of the room.

She'd marked a passage from the Psalms in yellow highlighter: *Some trust in chariots and some in horses, but we trust in the name of the Lord our God.*

Seth read it once, and then again, while the words burrowed deep into his soul. He'd done it again—thinking he knew better how to protect his family and taking the reins away from God.

Head bowed, arms resting on his knees, he loosened

his clenched fists and spread his hands, palms facing upward. It was both a gesture of release and of openness to receive whatever God offered. *I'm sorry, Lord. Sorry for fighting You for control. Sorry for trying to do things my way instead of trusting in Your perfect plan.*

"Daddy, are you sad?" Eva climbed into his lap and patted his cheek. "Omi said she wasn't mad at you."

"I know, sweetie. Daddy's just got a lot to think about right now." He snuggled his little girl close. "But don't you worry. Everything's going to be okay."

And it would be. Somehow, with God's help, it would be.

Christina sat for a long time in the shade of the oak tree while she tried to make sense of her emotions. Reason said she'd accomplished her purpose in coming to Juniper Bluff, which had always been to reestablish her independence. And God had used her here in other ways, too, not the least of which was helping a bright little boy and a precious little girl begin to move beyond the trauma of their past. She'd like to think she'd helped their dad, too, as Seth learned to laugh again while letting go of his own pain and guilt.

So it was time to move on...wasn't it? Lindsey Silva needed her back in Little Rock, where she could finally return to the work she'd trained for instead of cleaning bathrooms, making beds and sweeping floors.

Then why was it so hard? All she had to do was walk inside, find Marie and explain about Lindsey's call. She'd give two weeks' notice, plenty of time for the Petersons to find another housekeeper, and then pack her bags for Little Rock.

She stood, ready to do exactly that, but her legs

wouldn't cooperate. Halfway to the porch steps, she veered toward her cabin and didn't stop until she'd slammed the door behind her. Two steps ahead, Gracie halted and turned, head cocked and staring at Christina as if she'd lost her mind.

"Don't try to talk me out of this, Miss Know-It-All." Christina shook her finger at the dog. "You know it's the right thing to do."

If dogs could roll their eyes, Gracie just did. She gave Christina her backside, sauntered over to her doggy bed and plopped down.

"Fine, be that way." Christina crossed to the kitchenette and pulled sandwich fixings from the fridge. "And don't come begging for scraps from my lunch, either."

Her threat carried little weight, though, since her appetite dissipated before she'd taken three bites. With a resigned groan, she tore off pieces of bread crust and fed them to the dog.

Maybe she could clear her head by getting away from the ranch for a while. Armed with her grocery list, a chilled bottle of water and the novel she'd been reading, she loaded Gracie into the car and drove to town. After parking on a side street, she walked over to the square. The gazebo was deserted, so she climbed the steps and settled herself onto one of the benches lining the perimeter.

It was a warm afternoon, but the breeze felt good, carrying a sweet scent from the climbing roses adorning the gazebo, with a hint of fresh-mown grass mixed in. Gracie jumped up beside Christina and promptly fell asleep. One hand absently stroking the dog's head, Christina pulled out her paperback and prepared to lose herself in the adventures of a spunky heroine.

Far away in imaginary Paradise, Colorado, she took

little notice when someone joined her in the gazebo. A soft *ahem* made her look up, and she found Diana Matthews standing in front of her.

"Sorry to interrupt," Diana said, "but I was taking a break and saw you out here, so I thought I'd come over and say hi."

Christina laid the book aside. "Nice day, isn't it?"

"Not bad for the end of August." Sitting down next to Christina, Diana rested an elbow on the railing. "Slow week at the ranch?"

"Yes, but we should be full up for Labor Day weekend." Christina grazed her fingertips across the cover of her novel, wishing Diana would take the hint. Chatting with the woman who flirted so openly with Seth wasn't exactly comfortable.

Like you have any claim on him. You're planning to leave, remember?

"It's too bad about Seth, isn't it? Selling Tango—it breaks my heart." When Christina's shocked gaze met hers, Diana flinched. Her brows slanted in genuine concern. "You didn't know?"

Christina's throat closed. "He never said a word." Maybe because she'd blindsided him with her own news?

"I only found out because I was browsing equine message boards over lunch and his ad popped up. Looks like he just posted it this morning."

As if anticipating Christina's sudden eagerness to leave, Gracie jumped down and sat by the steps. Christina rose and stuffed her book into her purse. "Sorry, I have to go."

"Wait." Diana captured Christina's wrist. "If I've upset you, I apologize. It's just that I know what that horse means to Seth, and he would never sell her without good reason."

"Exactly, and that's what scares me." Staring hard at Diana, Christina wondered how much she dared confide in the woman. But she'd go crazy if she didn't talk this out with someone. "I'm afraid he's trying to cut ranch expenses. I've wondered for a while now how they can afford to keep paying me when they go for days at a time with no guest reservations."

Diana heaved a weary sigh. "The Petersons are good people, but sometimes their business sense isn't the sharpest. Serenity Hills has hardly changed in all the years they've been in operation. My dad has tried to convince them they need to modernize, but they're set on keeping things plain and simple, and that just won't cut it in the twenty-first century."

"But the regulars I've met this summer have told me the simplicity is exactly what brings them back." Christina shook her head, her voice falling to a reverent murmur. "I'd never want Serenity Hills to change. My time there has blessed me in ways I can't even describe."

Chapter Twelve

Inquiries about Tango began within hours of Seth's placing the online ads. To avoid Omi's stink-eye every time he answered the phone, he went looking for odd jobs to keep him occupied in and around the barn. Except there he had to keep out of his grandfather's way, because once Opi got wind of Seth's intentions, he'd lit into him like a bull on the rampage.

Like his grandparents had anything to worry about. Seth had set his asking price so high that after confirming, most callers politely hung up without requesting further details. Only two so far had expressed interest in coming out to see the horse, but Seth put them off until after the busy Labor Day weekend.

And maybe by then he could come up with some other idea that would make selling his prize mare unnecessary.

With all the cabins reserved for the holiday weekend, by Thursday morning preparations were in high gear. Omi enlisted Christina's help preparing menus, then sent Opi into Fredericksburg, where he could buy in bulk at one of the larger supermarket chains. Seth drove the riding lawnmower around the grounds, then spruced up the riding trails and picnic area. He preferred staying busy, especially these days, when every time he saw Christina, his chest ached like Tango had planted her hoof smack in the center of it.

He didn't think Christina had said anything to his grandparents yet about her plans to quit. Maybe she was holding off till after the holiday, too.

He was beginning to wish Labor Day weekend would last forever.

It almost felt like it did.

When Seth's clock radio blasted Alan Jackson in his ear at 5:45 a.m. Tuesday, he nearly pulverized it. The ranch was full up so seldom that he'd forgotten how much work it took to keep all those guests fed and entertained and out of trouble for three long days. Only an act of will propelled him out of bed for early-morning chores. Then a quick breakfast and off to school with Joseph. Even with the extra commitment involved, Seth was glad his son still got excited every morning about attending school with his friends.

Returning from town, Seth glimpsed Christina wrestling her maid's cart up the ramp to cabin three. She'd worked as relentlessly as any of them over the weekend, and no matter how hard he tried to stay angry at her for wanting to leave, he still cared.

It took him about two seconds to decide to swallow his pride and give her a hand. He slammed the pickup door, tossed his Stetson over the tailgate and marched down the hill to the cabins.

When he stepped inside, Christina looked up with a start. Dark circles shadowed her drooping eyes, and the smile she offered held no welcome. She flicked a strand of hair off her forehead. "Need something?"

"Thought you could use some help." He strode into the adjoining bathroom, where he started gathering up damp towels.

She stopped him in the doorway. "This is my job, not yours. Anyway, you must have a million other things to do."

"Nothing that can't—" The chirp of his cell phone interrupted him. With an apologetic shrug, he handed the towels to Christina and took the call. "Seth Austin."

"We spoke the other day," the male voice drawled. "If you haven't sold your horse yet, I'd still like to come out for a look-see."

A gust of air whistled between Seth's teeth. "Uh, sure. When did you have in mind?"

"I'm in San Antonio. Can't get there until later this afternoon, say around four?"

"Sounds good. I'll text you the directions." Ending the call, Seth grimaced as he thumb-typed the ranch's location into a text message.

A gentle touch to his arm made him look up. "Seth," Christina said, her gaze pleading, "don't do this. There has to be some other way."

Guess she found out he was selling Tango. "I'll do whatever it takes to keep Serenity Hills going. I owe it to my grandparents. I owe it to my kids."

"But what about you? What do *you* want, Seth?"

He faced her squarely, his throat aching with the words he longed to say: *I want you, Christina. I want you to stay right here with me and the kids for the rest of our lives.*

Instead, he hiked his chin and said, "The only thing I've ever wanted is what's best for my family. Like I said, I'll do whatever it takes." Sidling past her, he continued toward the door. "You're right, I've got some other stuff I need to do. Sorry to have bothered you."

He found his way blocked by a big yellow dog. Gracie sat between him and the porch steps, a funny kind of doggy-sneer baring her teeth. Seth never realized dogs were capable of so many facial expressions.

Christina came up beside him. "I'm pretty sure she doesn't want you to leave yet."

"I'm getting that message."

"So come sit down and let's talk, okay?" Taking his hand, Christina drew him over to the matching metal porch chairs. She tugged on his arm until he sat down next to her. "I've been wanting to say something ever since I ran into Diana in town—"

"Diana. Should have known." Staring up the hill, Seth tapped his boot heel.

"She's worried about you, too. And about Serenity Hills. Seth, she got me to thinking. This place has so much to offer, but it might be time to make some compromises."

Seth firmed his jaw. Compromise—wasn't that exactly what selling Tango would be? "I appreciate your concern, but you shouldn't worry about us." Forcing himself to meet her gaze, he offered his most convincing smile. "You've got your own life to live, Christina, and I'm happy you're getting another chance at the career you love and are clearly very good at." He stood abruptly. "Just don't wait too long to tell my grandparents you're leaving. They'll need time to make other arrangements."

And I'll need time to get you out of my heart.

This time, he didn't let Gracie stop him. Sidestepping the dog, he marched down the porch steps and straight for the barn. This might be his last day to spend with Tango, and he wanted to get one more good ride in.

As Christina watched Seth walk away, Gracie plodded over and rested her chin on Christina's lap. "I know, girl. But what can I do? He's got his mind made up."

And so do I.

Returning to Little Rock was the right thing to do, and not just because of Christina's career goals but for the sake of her hard-fought self-confidence. The weeks she'd spent at Serenity Hills had strengthened her both physically and emotionally. Yes, the work was still exhausting, but she no longer experienced such bone-deep fatigue or the debilitating muscle cramps that had plagued her when she first started pushing the heavy maid's cart up and down the hill.

The anxiety attacks were fewer and further between as well, which must account for Gracie's diminishing interest in being constantly on alert. The dog still seemed to know when Christina most needed her, but with each passing day Gracie acted more like a lovingly responsive pet than a service dog doing her job.

With the last of the towels and sheets dumped into the laundry bin and the cart replenished with supplies, Christina steeled herself for her conversation with Marie. Letting herself in the back door, she followed the sounds of clicking computer keys to the office down the hall.

"Marie?" Christina tapped on the open door. "Got a few minutes to talk?"

"Sure, hon, come on in." Turning away from the computer, Marie took a sip from her coffee mug. "There's a fresh pot in the kitchen if you want to grab a cup."

"No, thanks. I just need to get this said." Christina

sank onto the front edge of a chair, hands clasped in her lap. "I'll be going back to Little Rock soon. They need me at the social services office."

Marie slowly set down her mug. "We knew this day was coming, and I'm glad for you because I know it's what you want." She cast Christina a warm smile tinged with sadness. "But I can't say I'll be happy to see you go."

"And I'm grateful beyond measure for all the kindness you've shown me." She patted Gracie, lying beside the chair. "And my dog. Not everyone would be so understanding."

Rising, Marie circled the desk to give Christina a heartfelt hug. "Didn't I tell you from the start that your coming here was meant to be? Just look at all you've done for my Seth and his little ones. I never thought I'd see the day when Eva wouldn't run away in terror every time she saw a big dog. And Joseph *asking* to go to public school with his friends? You're a blessing to us all, honey."

Releasing a shaky laugh, Christina whisked wetness off her cheek. "Working here has blessed me, too, and Serenity Hills—all of you—will always hold a special place in my heart."

Marie eased down into the other chair, her brows drawing together in a worried frown. "Guess you've already told Seth you're leaving. That would explain why he's been so mopey lately." She harrumphed. "On top of his harebrained idea to sell Tango."

"He's only doing it because he thinks it'll help keep the ranch going, but…" Christina wondered how much she should say. After all, she was only an employee—not to mention an employee who'd just given notice. Chewing her lip, she began, "The other day, before things got so busy with the holiday weekend, I ran into Diana Matthews in town. She's the one who first told me about Seth selling Tango, and she also mentioned how her father has been saying you need to modernize."

"Figures." Marie pursed her lips. "But this wouldn't be Serenity Hills if we brought in all the trappings of the modern world. People come here to get away from all that."

"I agree. But if you're not getting enough reservations to pay the bills…"

"That's the crux of the matter. And even if reservations did pick up, Bryan and I are getting too old to work this hard and worry this much. We need to retire soon, and the only way I see that happening is if we sell the place." Mouth firm, Marie shook her head. "The problem is, Seth will fight us all the way."

Christina knew she spoke the truth. This ranch meant everything to Seth, so much that it had cost him his marriage and very nearly his children. "I'm so sorry, Marie. I wish I had answers for you."

"Aw, honey, you shouldn't be worrying about us." Almost the exact words Seth had spoken earlier, but coming from Marie they sounded sincere, not bitter. "And you go right ahead with your plans. I'll put the word out today about the job opening. Bet we get some calls by the end of the week."

While Marie marched around the desk and fired up her computer again, Christina sat a moment longer as she wrestled with her tangled feelings. Why did it suddenly hurt so much to think she could be so easily replaced? Did she really expect Marie to tell her she was the best housekeeper they'd ever had and drop to her knees to beg her to stay?

This was all for the best, right? Marie and Bryan

wanted to retire, anyway. Christina had noticed the brochure lying on the corner of the desk, information from a residential developer with enticing photos of fancy houses on lots large enough for a horse or two. Maybe the Petersons were already in negotiations to sell off part of the ranch. Christina hoped they'd leave the house, barn and a few choice acres for Seth and the children, because she couldn't imagine Seth being happy anywhere else.

The guy from San Antonio arrived earlier than expected, pulling to a stop near the barn only minutes after Seth returned from picking up Joseph at school. Sending Joseph into the house, Seth trudged over to meet Tango's prospective buyer.

Clad in crisp gray slacks and a dress shirt with loosened tie, the man looked less like a horseman than a banker or doctor. "Mr. Austin? I'm Greg O'Grady. Pleasure to meet you in person."

"You, too." Seth accepted O'Grady's firm handshake.

"Great place you have here." The man's gaze swept the pastures, cabins, lake and hills. "My family would love it."

"Happy to make a reservation for you anytime." Too keyed up to engage in small talk, Seth started around the side of the barn. "My horse is pastured back here."

O'Grady fell in step beside him. "If the photo in your ad does her justice, she's a real beauty."

"I'm proud of her."

"I can tell." An obvious dig at Seth's asking price. "You said you'd been training her for a while?"

"Several months. She's already placed in a couple of shows." Unlatching the pasture gate, Seth whistled for Tango. The mare trotted over, giving a snort as she nosed

Seth's palm in search of the treat he usually brought. "Sorry, girl, no peppermints this time."

"Gorgeous coloring." O'Grady ran a hand along Tango's neck. "Never seen a blue roan up close before."

Once again perusing the man's attire, Seth skewed his lips. "I expected you'd want to try her under saddle, but you wouldn't be doing those nice slacks and fancy loafers any favors."

O'Grady released an awkward chuckle. "Actually, my daughter's the rider in the family. She competes for her college, and I'd like to buy her an animal worthy of her skill."

"Generous dad." Apparently, the guy wasn't short on funds, which made this meeting all the more difficult. At least O'Grady hadn't driven up with a horse trailer in tow. Stifling a reluctant sigh, Seth offered to saddle up Tango and show the man what she could do.

By the time he rode her into the arena, his audience had multiplied. Omi, Opi and the kids joined O'Grady outside the fence, and while Seth's grandparents' politeness never wavered, their tight smiles didn't hide their disapproval of his decision. He couldn't hear their conversation, but it appeared O'Grady was asking a lot of questions, and *his* smile said a lot.

On Seth's next circuit of the arena, he noticed Opi nodding and grinning. O'Grady stuck out his hand, and Opi shook it briskly. Seth wouldn't hazard a guess as to what had so quickly turned them into best buds.

He halted at the fence, his tone stiff as he asked, "Anything else I can show you?"

"No, that's fine. She looks great."

Opi released the gate latch. "Take care of your horse and meet us in the house. We've got some jawin' to do."

Opi's confident smirk stirred jittery feelings in the pit of Seth's belly. What had they gone and done—sold Tango *and* Serenity Hills right out from under him?

While everyone else trekked to the house, Joseph hung back. "Can I help, Dad?"

"Sure. Grab the grooming tote." Seth clipped Tango in the cross-ties and removed the saddle. With Joseph plying a currycomb and Seth following up with a stiff brush, they quickly had Tango ready to return to her pasture.

Time to go find out what backdoor brokering had gone on between Greg O'Grady and Seth's grandparents. Seth glanced down at his son. "You hear much of what Opi and our visitor were talking about?"

"They talked some about the cabins. And I think maybe bringing some kids." Joseph shrugged. "I was watching you so I didn't pay much attention."

Cabins. And kids. Business for the ranch, maybe? Growing more anxious by the minute, Seth picked up his pace.

He found Omi in the kitchen pouring iced tea, while Eva perched on a barstool and arranged cookies on a plate. Opi and O'Grady sat talking at the table.

Omi motioned Seth over. "Go sit down. I think you'll want to hear what Greg has to say."

Already on a first-name basis, were they? Not at all sure he wanted to get in the middle of this, Seth took a chair at the far end of the table.

Opi shifted to face him. "Greg's got some real good ideas about how we could keep Serenity Hills going."

What Seth wanted to say was, *You figured all that out during a half-hour conversation?* Instead, he pasted on a neutral expression and murmured a vague "Oh?"

As Omi served iced tea and cookies, O'Grady animatedly described the work of a philanthropic organization he belonged to, one that specifically served the needs of disadvantaged children. "We've been looking to invest in a place like this, where the kids can experience nature and get away from their problems for a while."

Seth's brain immediately homed in on the word *invest*. He pushed his tea glass aside and sat forward. "What exactly did you have in mind, financially speaking?"

The more O'Grady talked, the more Seth liked what he was hearing. O'Grady's organization hoped to purchase or lease a facility where they could bring groups of children for weeklong stays throughout the summer and also for long weekends the rest of the year. "Obviously, additional staff would be necessary," O'Grady went on, "and we'd handle that area, as well."

Omi gripped Seth's hand. "It's an answered prayer, son. I really think we should consider what Greg's suggesting."

Gnawing the inside of his lip, Seth nodded slowly. "I admit, I'm intrigued. Yeah, put together a formal proposal and we'll talk."

"Wonderful! With your permission, I'll snap some photos while I'm here, and we'll discuss the possibilities at our next board meeting." O'Grady took another gulp of tea. "Now, about your horse..."

Seth's stomach plummeted. "To be honest, the only reason I offered her for sale was to help defray ranch expenses. But if this deal with your organization works out..."

"Yes, I see." Fingering his chin, O'Grady glanced away briefly. "Then how would you feel about a lease? I'd pay you to continue Tango's training, and my daughter could ride her in shows."

Opi hiked a brow. "It's the best of both worlds, Seth. What do you say?"

Seth rose and extended his hand to O'Grady. "I think my grandmother's right—your visit today is definitely the answer to several of our prayers."

O'Grady accepted Seth's handshake, and after they'd discussed a few more details, the man said his goodbyes. After Seth walked him out to his car and O'Grady drove away, Seth sighed and turned back toward the house. Looking past the garage, he glimpsed Christina walking Gracie down the lane, and his heart stammered.

Lord, You've been mighty good to me today, but there's one more prayer I have to ask. If there's any way You can fix things so Christina will stay, I'd be the happiest man alive.

Then an unnerving thought filled his mind: *If you truly love her, how much are you willing to sacrifice?*

His eyes fell shut as memories of Georgia intruded, along with the many things he'd refused to give up in order to save his marriage. He'd been as selfish and stubborn as Georgia, and they'd both paid the price.

But if he and the children followed Christina to Little Rock, could they ever adjust to city life? And who would help look after Omi and Opi, not to mention make sure Greg O'Grady's organization did right by Serenity Hills?

With the hectic Labor Day weekend, Seth hadn't made it to church on Sunday, but he'd been reading his Bible again, and a fragment from the passage he'd read in Joshua last night bloomed in his thoughts: *Be strong and courageous. Do not be afraid; do not be discouraged, for the Lord your God will be with you wherever you go.*

The promise resonated deep within him, lifting anxiety and restoring hope. It was long past time to forgive himself—and Georgia—for the mistakes they'd made. And maybe, God willing, there was still time to pursue a future with Christina.

With the cleanup after the holiday weekend behind her, Christina slept in on Wednesday. More guests weren't expected until Friday, and if things worked out as planned, within the next two weeks she'd be on her way home to Little Rock. The prospect of never again cleaning someone else's bathroom appealed mightily.

But the idea of never seeing Seth Austin again?

Leaning over the counter and the cup of coffee she'd just poured, she clutched her abdomen against the sharp, physical pain of already missing him. This was a complication she'd never planned on, and it scared her.

Gracie nosed beneath her arm and whimpered softly.

"I'll be okay, girl." She patted the dog's head and sank into the nearest chair. If she hoped to pick up where she left off at Child Protective Services, she *had* to be okay.

Except Gracie wasn't letting up. She bumped Christina's leg several times before laying her chin on Christina's thigh and staring up with pleading eyes.

Only then did Christina notice the tension in her limbs, the shortness of breath. She hadn't felt this agitated in so long that she'd almost forgotten the signs. When Gracie trotted to the bathroom and back, then paused expectantly at Christina's side, she realized she hadn't taken her medication this morning. At least Gracie had remembered.

"Thanks, girl. Guess I still need you more than I want to admit."

Gracie yipped and followed Christina to the bathroom, watching intently as if to be sure her mistress actually swallowed the pill.

Retrieving the coffee she'd all but forgotten, Christina warmed it in the microwave, then carried the mug to the front window. As Gracie plopped down beside her, a new thought intruded. It wouldn't be nearly as easy to go about her social worker duties with a service dog following her around. She might need to speak with Lindsey Silva about starting out with limited responsibilities until she felt ready to leave Gracie at home.

It was all just so aggravating. Christina was sick of being dependent on pills and lists, expecting others to be understanding of her condition and tolerant of her dog. She'd lived this way for two long years, and she was desperate for things to change, to return to life as she knew it before the accident.

Gracie emitted another whine and pushed against Christina's leg. She forced herself to inhale deeply and let the air out slowly. After a few more breaths, her agitation began to lessen, but before she could settle into a chair, a knock sounded on the door. She set down her mug to answer.

Seth stood on her porch. "Morning." He offered a hesitant smile. "Got time to talk?"

"Okay." Stepping aside, she invited him in. "I was just having coffee. Would you like a cup?"

"No, thanks." Seth's smile tightened. He glanced around uneasily.

Concern squeezed her chest. "Oh, Seth, did you sell Tango to that man yesterday?"

"Uh, not exactly." With a strange chuckle, he sank into one of the padded chairs in the sitting area.

She perched on the chair across from him. "Not exactly? I don't understand."

Disbelief tingeing his tone, he told her about the discussion he and his grandparents had had with Greg O'Grady. "We're still at the talking stage, but he sure got our hopes up about saving the ranch. With the additional staff they'd bring in, Opi and Omi could scale back their involvement, and getting the ranch on solid financial footing would ease Opi's stress level."

"Seth, it sounds like a perfect solution." A grateful tear trickled down Christina's cheek. "I'm so happy for you—and happy for all those children who'll get to experience Serenity Hills."

Seth sat forward, elbows on his knees and his gaze intense. "Christina, do you really have to go back to Little Rock?"

Breaking eye contact, she clutched Gracie's ruff. Then, realizing what the action signified, she slid her hand into her lap and stiffened her spine. "It's my career—my *life*. It's time to pick up the pieces and start living like a normal human being again."

"I get it, I really do." Seth nodded slowly, his Adam's apple bobbing with a hard swallow. "But…this thing between us… I just need to know if there's any hope it could be more."

"How, Seth? You'll be here, I'll be in Little Rock—"

"But what if I—"

"No, please." Christina pushed to her feet and crossed to the door. One hand on the knob, she stood to the side and tried to keep her voice steady. "Don't make this any harder than it already is."

It seemed an eternity before Seth finally got up to leave. When he halted in front of Christina, his mouth worked as if he might say more, but then he squared his shoulders and marched out without a backward glance.

A sob rose in Christina's throat, and she stifled it with

a hand to her mouth. She couldn't stay, and she wouldn't in a million years ask Seth to leave behind the home that meant everything to him. Now, especially, with the possibility of infusing new life into the ranch, he had even more reason to stay and see it through.

Chapter Thirteen

Only two cabins were occupied the following weekend, which meant less work for Christina but more time to fill as she waited out her last days at Serenity Hills. Avoiding Seth became a top priority, because each time their gazes met, she could see the longing in his eyes…and she had no confidence she could hide her own tumultuous feelings from him.

Late Tuesday morning, as Christina inventoried supplies in the storeroom, she heard a car drive up. Peeking out the door, she recognized the dark blue SUV belonging to the man who'd come out to see Tango last week. Had Mr. O'Grady returned with further plans for investing in Serenity Hills? Christina sent up a prayer that the news would be good.

Now, where had she left off? Consulting her supply list, she couldn't remember how many miniature shampoo bottles she'd just counted, so she started over. After finishing with the toiletries, she moved on to coffee packets. Marie would need to place another order with their supplier soon.

As she checked off the last item on the list, voices outside drew her attention. A few seconds later, the Petersons stepped in, followed by their visitor. Seth entered last, Eva perched on his hip.

"Don't mean to interrupt," Marie said with a warm smile.

"All done." Christina hung the clipboard in its spot on one of the cabinet doors. "I'll get out of your way."

"No need to rush off. Christina, I'd like you to meet Greg O'Grady." Marie's smile broadened. "Looks like we're about to partner with Greg's organization."

Christina offered her hand to the well-dressed gentleman. "Seth told me about your ideas for opening Serenity Hills to disadvantaged children. I think it's a wonderful plan."

"Our board is very excited to get things rolling," Mr. O'Grady replied. "I understand you won't be staying on, though."

Christina shot a quick glance at Seth and Eva, concern for the little girl pricking her heart. She lowered her voice. "No, I can't. I have a job waiting for me back in Little Rock."

"Really sorry to hear that. Seth mentioned you have a lot of experience with children."

"Yes, I was—am—a child and family social worker." When Gracie eased her head beneath Christina's palm, she checked herself for signs of anxiety. All this talk about leaving Serenity Hills and the fact that she wouldn't be a part of the changes in store had definitely affected her. But she wouldn't be human if she didn't feel some sense of loss over the friendships she'd made here.

Friendships. Right.

When Bryan suggested they continue the tour of the property, Mr. O'Grady wished Christina well and followed the Petersons out. Seth turned to leave as well, but Eva reached out to Christina.

A big, wet tear slipped from the little girl's eye. "I don't want you to go away!"

"Oh, honey." Christina lifted Eva from Seth's arms and snuggled her close. Fighting tears of her own, she couldn't even look at Seth. "I have to go because there are other children who need my help. But I promise I will never, ever forget you. You're more special to me than you can ever know."

Seth gently extracted his daughter from Christina's embrace. His cheek tucked against Eva's golden curls, he cast Christina an apologetic frown. "Hadn't had a chance to break the news to the kids yet. Guess I was stalling as long as possible."

She stroked Eva's back. "I'm sorry, too."

Marie peeked into the storeroom. "There you are, Seth. Thought you were right behind us." She glanced at Christina, and her expression filled with sympathy. With an understanding smile, she reached for Eva. "You better come with me, sweet thing. Daddy'll be along shortly."

As Marie's footsteps faded, Christina hugged her arms across her middle and hoped Seth would make a quick exit, as well.

He didn't. "How many ways do I have to say it, Christina? I'm crazy about you, and so are the kids. Say you'll stay. Or let us be with you in Little Rock. Whatever it takes—"

"Seth, please—"

In two quick strides he closed the space between them. With one hand at her waist, the other clasping her nape, he kissed her, driving all other thoughts from her mind.

Time stopped on a tide of confusing emotions, and when her muscles went limp, she clung to him for fear of falling.

Some distant part of her gave a cynical, mocking laugh, because she'd already fallen way too hard. *And if you don't end this now, you'll never be able to leave.*

Forcing her palms against his chest, she pushed him away. "Seth, stop." Her words came out in a shaky gasp. "Please. We can't do this."

He gripped her shoulders, his breathing ragged. "Why not? Because if you have any feelings at all for me—and I'm convinced you do—I know we can work this out."

"No, we can't." If Seth wouldn't see things realistically, then Christina would have to take a stand for both their sakes. She edged toward the doorway, giving Seth her back. "I'll be leaving on Monday as soon as I finish cleaning the cabins. If it's okay with you, I'd like some time with the children on Sunday evening so I can tell them goodbye."

When he didn't answer right away, she dared a glance over her shoulder. Chin down, fists planted against his hips, Seth looked as if he struggled for control. Only then did Christina notice Gracie hadn't followed her to the door. The dog padded over to Seth, sat down beside him, and leaned hard against his leg until he relaxed his stance and knelt to pet her.

He looked up at Christina, and a bittersweet smile nudged at the corners of his mouth. "Don't know who I'll miss more—you or this supersmart dog."

His remark eased the tension between them, and Christina turned with a soft laugh. "I'll miss you, too, Seth—you know I will. But please tell me you understand why it has to be this way."

With another pat to Gracie's head, he stood. "The logical part of me does. The rest…not so much." He heaved a weary shrug. "Guess I should catch up with the ranch tour. Life goes on."

"Yeah," Christina murmured as he slipped past her and out the door. "Life goes on."

Catching up with his grandparents and O'Grady, Seth needed a bucketful of willpower to keep his mind on business when everything in him ached to race back to Christina and find some way to convince her they could be together. Juniper Bluff, Little Rock, Timbuktu—the *where* didn't matter anymore.

But something told him he'd pushed hard enough, and the only thing left to do was leave his future—and Christina's—in God's hands.

As they strolled through the barn, another car drove up. O'Grady had said three other board members would be meeting him here to see the place and bring their thoughts to the discussion. Two men and a woman, all dressed in business attire—but wearing sensible shoes, at least— stepped from the sedan. O'Grady made the introductions, then chimed in with his observations while Seth's grand-parents continued showing the board members around.

After the tour, Omi invited everyone in for sand-wiches. The conversation continued over lunch, then cof-fee and Omi's homemade pecan pie. Mrs. Locker, the board chairperson and an affable woman in her midfif-ties, assured Seth and his grandparents that they wouldn't have to turn their longtime regulars away.

"Our current vision," Mrs. Locker explained, "is to bring a different group of children for a weeklong stay every two or three weeks over the summer, then probably one weekend a month during the school year."

"The schedule would be established well in advance," O'Grady added. "So you'll always know which dates are open for other reservations."

Opi nodded. "Sounds fair."

The discussion turned to money and staffing. Mrs. Locker stated they already had an attorney drafting various contractual details and suggested Seth and his grandparents engage their own attorney to ensure their interests were protected. By the time Seth excused himself to pick up Joseph from school, he was feeling more and more confident, not only about the future of Serenity Hills but about the positive effect of this arrangement on Opi's health and Omi's peace of mind.

His biggest concern now was his kids, because ever since Eva found out Christina would be deserting them, she'd latched on to Seth as if *he* were the one planning to leave.

Okay, maybe *deserting* was too strong a word. Seth had to keep reminding himself Christina had always implied her employment here was only temporary. The pain he felt now was his own fault for letting himself fall in love with her.

Eva whimpered and sniffled all the way to town. Every time Seth glanced at her through the rearview mirror, his heart tripped. Her button nose had turned a bright shade of pink, and her eyes were puffy from crying. Seth could only pray his little girl's hard-fought sense of security would survive this blow.

And his son's as well, he thought as he merged into the line of cars in front of Joseph's school. Both his kids had come so far in the last few weeks. He couldn't let either of them suffer a setback. Maybe Omi was right and Seth needed to reconsider getting the children into counseling. Hadn't the years since Georgia's death proved his own efforts futile in providing Joseph and Eva the help they needed? And getting to know Christina had certainly shown him not all social workers were cut from the same cloth.

He thumped the steering wheel. *Please, God, don't take Christina out of our lives.*

The school bell clanged, and within minutes a horde of children stampeded through the main doors. Seth spotted Joseph in the crowd, the boy's black-and-silver backpack crammed full and sagging from his shoulders. Most likely a new batch of library books and a lunchbox reeking with the remains of the raw veggies neither Seth nor Omi could convince him to eat.

Waving to some friends, Joseph yanked open the rear passenger door and climbed into the pickup. "Hey, Dad! Hey, Eva—What's wrong? Why are you crying?"

Before Seth could intervene, Eva blurted out, "Miss Christina's going away!"

"Huh?" Joseph shot his father a panicked look. "No way!"

Seth should have instructed Eva not to say anything, but he'd been too distracted by his own jumbled thoughts. "Buckle up, son," he said as the parent in the car behind him gave an impatient honk. "I'll explain on the way home."

He barely made it off school property before Joseph hammered him with questions. "Why, Dad? Where's she going? Doesn't she like us anymore?"

Meanwhile, Eva's sobs grew louder, until Seth thought his chest would explode. "Cool it, both of you!" He slammed on the brakes to keep from running down the school crossing guard who'd just stepped into the street.

"Let me get out of traffic, okay? I promise, I'll tell you everything."

Now he had to listen to Joseph's sniffles along with Eva's hiccupping swallows. He'd like to pull over to the side of the road and let loose his own crying jag, for all the good it would do. On the other hand, pulling off the road until he regained some control seemed like a wise idea. Coincidentally—or not—they were coming up on the very spot where Seth had first met Christina, the day he'd waved her to a stop so he could rescue the turtle.

He steered to the curb, lowered the windows and shut off the engine. Unbuckling his seat belt, he twisted around to face his kids in the back seat. "I know this is hard, and I'm as sad as you are. But there are lots of other families who need Miss Christina, and she's happiest when she's helping kids out of bad situations or showing moms and dads how to be better parents."

Joseph's chin trembled. "Like she did for us?"

"Exactly." Seth patted his son's knee. "So we need to be brave and let her go where she's most needed, right? Because we love her and want what's best for her."

"But what about us?" Eva whined. "We need her, too."

Oh, boy, did they! Seth pressed his eyes shut while he hauled in a steadying breath. Opening his eyes, he looked sternly at each of his children. "Do you trust Jesus?"

Sharing a glance with each other, both Joseph and Eva nodded solemnly.

"Well, I do, too, and I believe He's going to work everything out for our very best and for Christina's. Maybe it means we'll have to miss her for a while, maybe forever—" His throat closed, and he had to glance away.

"Like Mommy?" Joseph murmured.

Seth swung his head around. "No. Not like Mommy.

This is different, son. *I'm* different." He gripped Joseph's hand, then Eva's. "All of us, we're stronger now. Wiser. And because God brought Christina to us just when we needed her most, we know how much God loves us, don't we?"

Both children nodded.

"So we can trust that no matter what the future brings, He's not letting go of us. We'll get through this. We'll be fine." He spoke to reassure his children, but also to convince himself. Lifting the console cover, he grabbed handfuls of tissues and passed them back to the kids. After giving their chins loving tweaks, he faced forward and buckled up. "Let's get on home now, and when you see Miss Christina, I want you to give her big smiles and hugs and let her know that no matter how far apart we are, she'll always be our special friend."

He nearly choked on the word *friend*. He'd wanted more, so much more. *Lord, if it's Your will, help us find a way.*

Checking on his kids in the rearview mirror several times on the way home, Seth couldn't be prouder of how they fought to pull themselves together. Joseph clutched Eva's hand, offering brotherly encouragement with gentle words and tender glances that barely disguised his own dismay.

As they neared the ranch turnoff, Seth peered over his shoulder to offer one more bit of reassurance before the kids had to face Christina. "Now remember—"

"Dad!" Joseph's terrified gaze fixed on something ahead. "Watch out!"

After her encounter with Seth in the storeroom that morning, Christina decided to stay close to her cabin and avoid further damage to her shattering heart. A headache had mushroomed in her right temple, and two doses of migraine pills had barely put a dent in it. She could probably blame the emotional tension, which she hoped would ebb as soon as she returned to Little Rock and the work she missed so desperately.

Gracie must have sensed the tension, as well. She'd hardly stopped pacing all afternoon, wearing a trench in the floorboards between the front door and the sofa, where Christina reclined with an ice pack pressed to her throbbing head.

It was both touching and heartrending to recall how Gracie had deserted Christina to comfort Seth earlier. To realize the dog had sensed Seth needed consolation so much more than Christina did in that moment—how could she doubt the depth of his feelings for her?

God, help me! I don't want to hurt him. I don't want to hurt Joseph and—

The blare of horns and a metallic crash, sounds both familiar and frightening, penetrated her headache-induced fog. The ice bag fell to the floor as she sat up with a start. *Haley's shotgun-wielding father. The screech of tires. The sickening crunch as the unseen dump truck slammed into her.*

Then Gracie's frantic whining. A wet tongue sweeping across Christina's face. Awareness returning, she struggled to her feet. The rational part of her brain registered that Seth usually picked up Joseph from school around this time. "Please, God, no!"

She charged out the door, while her imagination conjured up nightmarish images of Seth's pickup turned to a mass of twisted metal, his and Joseph's mangled bodies sprawled amid the wreckage. The distance from her cabin to the lane stretched into eternity, and the faster she ran, the more her feet seemed mired in quicksand.

She reached the Petersons' back porch at the same moment Marie rushed out. Marie grabbed her shoulders. "Slow down, honey. Everything's under control. The sheriff and EMS are on their way."

Christina fought for breath as she struggled to see past the woman to the road beyond. "Is it Seth? Is he hurt?"

Marie took too long to answer, her own gaze swinging toward the road.

Christina broke free and willed her legs into motion once more. Vaguely aware of Marie's thudding footfalls behind her, she bolted past the house and pastures. Up ahead, where the ranch drive ended at the main road, she glimpsed a dark SUV resting nose-down in the ditch. Smoke billowed from under the hood. Beyond the SUV, a green pickup pulling a horse trailer sat crossways in the road.

A green pickup. Not maroon.

Not Seth's.

Halting several feet away, pulse thrumming in her ears, Christina sank to her knees. Gravel bit into the thin skin over her kneecaps, but she hardly felt it. Reaching instinctively for the dog never far from her side, she sank her fingers deep into Gracie's fur and drew sharp, gasping breaths.

She felt Marie's hand on her shoulder, and she looked up to see Bryan striding their way. He held tight to Joseph's and Eva's hands. Praise God they appeared physically unscathed, but shock and confusion filled their eyes.

Eva broke free and ran straight for Christina, her little body wrapping around Christina's like a boa constrictor. "We nearly wrecked. It was so scary!"

Still in shock, Christina couldn't find her voice. She held Eva close while straining for a glimpse of Seth. If the kids weren't hurt, he should be okay, too…shouldn't he?

But where was he?

Then she saw him. Emerging from the horse trailer, he carefully led a limping horse to the side of the road. Another man followed with a second horse, this one with blood streaming down its rear leg.

"Keep an eye on the kids," Bryan said, speaking to Marie. "I'm gonna fix up a couple of stalls in the barn where the horses can stay until Doc Ingram checks them out."

As the wail of sirens grew louder, Marie helped Christina to her feet. "Let's take the kids to the house. They don't need to be out here for this." Concern deepened the lines around her eyes. "And neither do you."

With Gracie on one side, Marie and the children on the other, she reluctantly turned her back on the crash scene and the man who'd claimed her heart.

Chapter Fourteen

"Here, drink this." Marie set a steaming cup of herbal tea in front of Christina. It smelled like chamomile.

She hadn't stopped shaking, even with Marie's plush crocheted afghan wrapped around her shoulders and Gracie curled up at her feet.

Joseph turned from the front window, where he'd been keeping watch ever since they came inside. "The tow trucks just left. Dad and Opi are coming up the lane."

A few minutes later, the back door swung open and Seth clomped into the kitchen. He looked hot, dirty and exhausted. He flung his Stetson toward the hat rack and missed, then ignored it and went straight to the fridge for a canned soft drink.

"Will those horses be all right?" Marie asked.

"Looks like it. Opi's out there with the owner and Doc Ingram." Seth's gaze met Christina's, and a look of comprehension darkened his features. He set down his drink and strode to the table to kneel at her side. "Baby, are you okay?"

She started to nod, then shook her head rapidly. "No… no, I'm not okay." Throwing her arms around his neck, she clung to him with a ferocity to match Eva's hold on her only an hour ago. "I was so scared. I thought you were—"

"I'm fine." Easing back far enough to look deeply into her eyes, he took her hand and placed it on his cheek. "See? Not a scratch."

His day's growth of whiskers rasped against her palm. His gaze, so full of love and reassurance, made her choke back a sob.

Rising, he snugged the afghan around her. "You should rest. Let me take you back to your cabin."

"No, I want to stay with you." She latched on to his hand.

He pulled a chair closer and sat facing her. "I'm right here, Christina. I won't leave your side."

She nodded weakly, shame filling her. She was supposed to be getting stronger, not falling apart like this. Not days before she should be starting back to work at Child Protective Services.

Eva appeared at Seth's side and tugged on his shirtsleeve. "Is Miss Christina sick?"

"She had a bad scare, sugar. I'm gonna take care of her." He planted a kiss on Eva's head, then turned to his son, who now leaned on the windowsill to watch the goings-on at the barn. "Joseph, take your sister in the other room and read her a story, okay?"

"Aw, Dad, I wanna see—"

"Now, Joseph. Please."

As the children trudged out of the kitchen, Marie brought Seth's soft drink to the table and handed him a moist washcloth. "This'll help cool you off."

Watching beads of perspiration slip down Seth's temples, Christina thought how odd it was that she should feel so cold. With a shaky breath, she reached for her mug of tea and took a careful sip. Seth offered a smile of approval, then gulped from his frosty soda can.

Marie slumped into a chair at the other end of the table. "What exactly happened out there, Seth? Did they figure out who was at fault?"

"Looks like O'Grady will be ticketed for distracted driving. Said he was trying to answer a cell phone call and didn't see the other guy." As Seth described the accident, Christina couldn't keep herself from listening. At Joseph's warning, Seth had barely stopped in time to miss Greg O'Grady's SUV as the man pulled out onto the road. O'Grady had swerved straight into the path of the oncoming pickup pulling the horse trailer, then overcorrected and landed in the ditch. When the pickup driver braked, the trailer jackknifed. O'Grady's air bag saved him from anything more serious than a bloody nose and bruised ribs. The man pulling the trailer suffered a bruised shoulder, and one of his horses would need a leg wound sewn up.

"Oh, my," Marie said. "It could have been so much worse."

The woman's words, though spoken softly, launched an eruption of panic inside Christina. Her heart thundered in her chest, and she couldn't catch a full breath. The half-empty cup slipped from her fingers, spilling tea across the table before it teetered on the edge and splintered on the tile floor.

Gracie skittered out of the way as both Seth and Marie hurried over. "That settles it," Marie stated, bundling Christina into her arms. "You're staying in our guest room tonight, sweetie, and I'm taking you upstairs to tuck you in right now."

She hadn't the strength to argue, and she wasn't sure

she wanted to. Even with Gracie at her side, she didn't think she could bear staying alone in the cabin. *Dear God, this can't be happening again!*

Marie guided her toward the hallway. "Honey, do you have some medicine you can take, something to calm your nerves and help you rest?"

"My pills…in the medicine cabinet."

"Seth, go see what she's got over there. And get back here lickety-split."

Seth wasted no time jogging over to Christina's cabin. He found several prescription bottles in the bathroom and grabbed them all. Then it occurred to him that Christina might not be coherent enough to know which pills to take, or remember what she'd already taken today so she didn't overdose.

Debating whether to call the doctor listed on the prescription bottles, he spotted Christina's cell phone on the coffee table and on a whim tried the health info icon. A list of emergency contact numbers appeared on the screen. He pressed the call button for the top name, Christina's parents.

Her mother answered almost immediately. "Chrissy! How are you, sweetie?"

Seth cringed, dreading how his news would upset the woman. "Ma'am, it's Seth Austin. I'm sorry, but we've got a problem here."

As he explained the situation, Mrs. Hunter's anxious gasps sounded in his ear. "Oh, poor Chrissy. I've been expecting a call like this ever since she went to work for you."

Bristling at her comment, Seth struggled to keep his

tone polite. "Until today, she was doing great. If you'll just tell me how we can help her, I'm sure—"

"*I'm* sure this is beyond your level of expertise. What's your nearest major airport?"

"San Antonio, but—"

"Christina's father and I will be on the soonest possible flight. Give me a number where we can call for directions after we rent a car."

All Seth could think about was how hard Christina had worked to regain her independence. If her parents swooped in now to rescue her, it could mean an even worse setback. "Mrs. Hunter, please don't come. Give her a chance to pull out of this on her own."

"Christina is our daughter, and she needs us!" The woman's pitch and volume climbed with every word. "How can you even suggest we stay away?"

"You want what's best for her, don't you?" Seth pinched the bridge of his nose as he searched for the right words. "I'm a parent, too, and believe me, I understand how badly you want to help and protect Christina. But there comes a time in every parent-child relationship when you've got to let go and trust God."

Mrs. Hunter sniffed. "I know… I know," she replied, her tone softening. "And I do trust God. But we love Chrissy so much, and after all she's been through, how can we not worry?"

Seth had no answer, because even as he got better at loosening his grip on his own children, he still couldn't completely shut down the worry factor. "Tell you what. I'll read off these prescription labels and you tell me what Christina should be taking. Let's see how she does between now and tomorrow morning. You can always come later if she needs you."

A pause. "You'll call me right away if she gets worse?"

"Of course. But let's pray that doesn't happen."

Armed with Mrs. Hunter's instructions about Christina's medications, Seth tucked the phone into his pocket and sprinted back to the house. After a quick check on the kids, still reading together in the family room, Seth headed upstairs. In the guest room, his grandmother had pulled a rocking chair close to the bed where Christina shivered under a quilt. Gracie snuggled close beside her, chin resting on her paws and eyes alert with unmistakable concern.

Seth signaled Omi to join him in the hallway, then handed her the prescription bottles as he related his phone call with Mrs. Hunter.

Omi studied the labels. She kept one vial out, then stuffed the rest into her pocket. "Fetch a glass of water."

Once they convinced Christina to swallow the pills, it wasn't long before the shivering subsided and she drifted into what Seth hoped would prove restful sleep.

He doubted he'd sleep at all until he knew Christina would be okay.

When evening neared, he sat with Christina while his grandmother cobbled together a light supper of leftovers for the family. She brought a plate up to Seth, but he only picked at his food. Mostly he just watched Christina and prayed.

Later, the kids asked to peek in before getting ready for bed. When Eva stood on tiptoe to kiss Christina's forehead, she barely stirred. Giving Gracie a hug, Eva whispered, "You take good care of her, okay, girl?"

The dog responded with a tongue-swipe across Eva's hand, then scooted deeper into the curve of Christina's body.

Seth wished he had a right to do the same, to cradle and comfort and encourage the woman he grew to love more every day.

Morning brought little change. Christina roused long enough to swallow her medications and for Seth's grandmother to coax a little warm broth down her throat. Then she slept again. Seth dutifully phoned Mrs. Hunter with a report and once again pleaded for more time. The woman reluctantly agreed, provided Seth promised to call regularly.

Ranch chores and getting Joseph to and from school kept Seth occupied for a good part of the day, but he looked in on Christina every chance he got. When he went upstairs after lunch, he found Eva sitting in the rocking chair with a big storybook on her lap and reading to Christina. She wasn't getting all the words right, but the familiar fairy tale didn't lose much in translation.

Even better, Christina was awake. She'd propped her head up on a couple of pillows, and with one arm draped across Gracie's back, she seemed enthralled by Eva's story.

The scene moved Seth so deeply that he didn't have the heart to intrude.

Later, Omi encouraged Christina to eat a few bites of chicken noodle soup, after which she drifted back to sleep. Once he'd tucked the children into bed, Seth called Mrs. Hunter to report that her daughter had had a peaceful day.

On Thursday, Omi came up with a long list of jobs that needed to be handled before a family of four arrived for the weekend. For a change, Seth was glad they hadn't had more bookings. He and his grandfather took care of freshening the cabin, then Omi sent Opi to town for groceries.

At lunch, Seth asked if he could take Christina's tray up to her. He breathed a sigh of gratitude to find her on the love seat beneath the window, a Bible on her lap and Gracie snuggled at her side.

Her eyes brightened when she saw him in the doorway. "Hi, stranger."

"Hi, yourself." Seth entered and set the tray on the nightstand. "How are you feeling?"

"Like a slug. Honestly, I'm not even sure what day it is."

"It's Thursday. You've pretty much slept away the past couple of days."

Chin dropping, she lifted a hand to her forehead. "I'm so sorry for bringing you and your grandparents into my drama."

"It's okay. You couldn't help it." Seth sank onto the other end of the love seat. "I'm just glad you're feeling better."

With a quick intake of breath, Christina whisked away a tear. "Not as better as I ought to be by now. I feel so— so—" Her gaze swept the ceiling. "Weak. Incompetent. A complete and utter failure."

"That's ridiculous." When Seth leaned over to scoop her into his arms, Gracie slid to the floor to keep from getting squashed. Seth ran his hand tenderly up and down Christina's spine as she wept against his chest. "You had a bad scare, that's all. This isn't permanent, Chrissy. You'll get through it."

She tipped her head to shoot him an accusatory frown. "Nobody calls me Chrissy but my parents. You called them, didn't you?"

He winced. "Guilty." With a sheepish grin, he pressed a kiss to her temple. "Don't blame a guy for doing everything he can to take care of the woman he's falling crazy in love with."

"Oh, Seth…" She buried her face deep in the crook of his shoulder, her whole body shaking with smothered tears.

Had he said too much? These probably weren't the best circumstances for professing the depth of his feelings, but he wanted her to know. Maybe if she realized how serious he was about being there for her, about wanting to spend the rest of his life with her—

"Christina," he murmured against her hair, "I know you're not feeling very strong right now, but you've pulled through before and you'll do it again. And believe me when I say that nothing in your past, your present or your future will ever change how much I love you. If you'll let me, I want to walk this journey with you, every step of the way."

Long seconds passed before her head bobbed in an acquiescent nod. She straightened and brushed the wetness from her cheeks. "I love you, too, Seth—you must know I do. But I'm so confused now. I need time to think."

"Take all the time you need. I'll be here." He wanted to kiss her so badly right now, but he held back. Instead, he reached for the tray. "How about some lunch?"

Confusion didn't begin to encompass Christina's jumbled feelings. High on the list were disillusionment and regret, followed close behind by guilt and shame. What hubris to believe two months of independent living could negate the trauma that two *years* of therapy, daily meds and the help of a service dog had really only masked?

She'd stubbornly refused to accept her doctor's often repeated reminders that the complications of her head injury would likely cause issues for the rest of her life. Yes, with continued counseling and the passage of time, she might expect the PTSD to abate. Not so with the headaches, mood swings, occasional forgetfulness and a whole list of other annoying complaints.

It wasn't fair—it simply wasn't fair! Since her earliest memories she'd been drawn to the care of children. When playing with neighbor kids or the cousins who visited often, she always wanted to be the mother, the schoolteacher, the kindly doctor or nurse. As a teenager, she quickly proved herself a reliable and conscientious babysitter, turning down far more jobs than she could fit into her schedule.

Now, to lose forever the career she'd invested all her efforts to achieve, the work that fulfilled her like nothing else ever had—*why, God?*

And Seth, dear Seth. She'd fallen so hard for this man that just a glimpse of his quirky smile could take her breath away. But she'd denied that, too, at first because with their disparate goals in life she didn't see how they could ever be together. And now...because she couldn't bear the thought of burdening him with a lifetime of dealing with her weakness, her neediness, her infirmity.

She kept him at arm's length for the rest of the day, and he seemed to accept her need for space. After another night in the Petersons' guest room, she awoke Friday morning to the unmistakable smell of smoldering mesquite. Realizing Bryan must have fired up the smoker to barbecue for ranch guests, she suffered a different kind of guilt. Here she was, lazing in bed like pampered royalty while others assumed her housekeeping duties.

Throwing aside the covers, she thrust her feet to the floor. "Come on, Gracie, we've convalesced long enough."

After freshening up in the bathroom, she changed from Marie's borrowed pajamas into the shorts and T-shirt she'd worn three days ago.

Marie met her on the stairs, breakfast tray in hand. "Where do you think you're going, young lady?"

"If I continue hiding away up here, I'll go crazy—" Christina grimaced. "Crazier than I already am, anyway."

"Now, honey—"

"It's okay," Christina interrupted with a forced laugh. "I'm kidding…mostly. Anyway, I need to be doing something. I need to feel—" An unexpected sob choked off the rest of her words.

Marie paused for only a second before doing a quick about-face and marching downstairs. Over her shoulder, she said, "All righty, then, come on to the kitchen and have some breakfast first. Afterward, there's plenty to do, and I'm happy to put you to work."

Christina could kiss the woman for being so understanding.

She also appreciated that Marie assigned small but necessary kitchen jobs—peeling carrots, chopping peppers, supervising Eva as she spooned cookie dough onto baking sheets—tasks that kept Christina busy without overtaxing her strength.

Whenever Seth's duties brought him through the kitchen, he shared a smile and an encouraging nod but maintained his distance. Even so, Christina sensed his watchful eye and unspoken concern.

By Saturday, she felt much stronger physically, if still on the shaky side emotionally. When Marie sent Seth down to the lake to set up for the evening picnic, Christina offered her help.

"Are you sure?" Seth asked, a twist to his mouth.

With a mock scowl, she set her fists at her waist. "Is that a critique of my bluebonnet centerpieces?"

Her remark evoked the hoped-for laugh, along with a relieved grin. "Wouldn't dream of insulting your centerpieces."

Working alongside Seth to spread tablecloths and arrange candles and silk flowers felt good. Felt right. When they finished, Seth took her hand and led her down to the lakeshore. "It's a gorgeous day. Let's just sit for a while, okay?"

"Are you sure you have time?"

"Plenty." He plopped onto the grass and drew her down beside him. They sat facing the lake, knees drawn up and elbows hooked around their knees.

Neither spoke for several minutes, and Christina savored the silence, interspersed with birdcalls and the splash of water lapping the shore. And, of course, Gracie's snuffling snores as she dozed next to Christina. The poor dog had to be exhausted after the past few days.

Then, barely above a whisper, Seth asked, "Are you still planning to leave after the weekend?"

The question caught her so off guard that she laughed out loud. "Of all the things weighing on my mind since Tuesday, would you believe leaving *wasn't* one of them?"

He looked at her askance. "What—not once?"

Slowly, she shook her head. "I'm not sure when it happened, but sometime between Tuesday and today I realized I don't want to leave. Not anymore." A knot formed in her chest. "There's nothing for me in Little Rock now—

except for my mom and dad, anyway. I was foolish to think I could ever go back to the way things were."

"No, not foolish." Seth shifted closer, pulling her against his side. "Just hopeful. And no one can blame you for that."

"Yes, I was hopeful." Cynicism crept into her tone. "But utterly unrealistic. Now I don't know what to do with myself. Am I supposed to simply give up and let other people take care of me for the rest of my life?"

Seth's chest rose and fell as he gazed across the serene surface of the lake. "What if there were three people who desperately needed *you* to help take care of *them*?"

"I do love you, Seth. And I love Joseph and Eva and your grandparents, too." Wrapped in the circle of his embrace, she trembled. "But can't you see? I'm a mess. You have no idea what you'd be signing up for."

"The only mess I see is the one you'll leave behind if you walk out on what we have." When she gave her head a violent shake, he took her by the shoulders and made her look at him. "Baby, I get it. You've just been forced to say goodbye to your lifelong dream—or at least what you *thought* was your dream. But there are other ways to fill that big ol' hole in your heart. And I don't mean just by marrying a grumpy cowboy with two kids and a guest ranch."

"Marry—?" Her mouth fell open.

He rambled on as if she weren't staring at him like a gaping fish. "Did you already forget what I told you about O'Grady's proposal? Think of all the opportunities you'll have for working with disadvantaged kids— kids who could really benefit from your knowledge and experience."

As the possibilities swam through her brain, excitement grew. Could this be God's answer to her prayer, a chance that she could yet make a difference in the lives of disadvantaged children?

Then her thoughts converged once again on a single word: *marry.* "Seth, did you really just say—"

Something big and furry bumped against her back, and she tumbled into Seth's arms. Barking wildly, tail wagging, Gracie pranced in circles around them, and Christina could only laugh at her silly dog's antics.

Seth's laughter mingled with hers for a sparkling moment before he froze and gazed into her eyes. His grin widened. "Yes, Christina Hunter, you heard me right. I'm asking you to marry me, and I won't take no for an answer."

Tears sprang to her eyes. "Would you accept a 'yes, but'?"

He hiked a brow. "Depends on what comes after the *but.*"

"*But* only if you come to Little Rock with me—just for a visit. I want my parents to meet you, and I want you to come with me to see my doctor." Smiling into his eyes, she caressed his cheek. "I want to make sure you know exactly what you're getting into."

"Yes to all your conditions," he said, "but I guarantee you they won't make one bit of difference. I'm in this for the long haul, and with God—and Gracie—keeping both of us on track, we can't go wrong."

As if to prove him right, Gracie pawed his arm and whined until he shoved her away and swept Christina into a kiss that rocked her to her toes. Lingering in his embrace, she recalled the words Marie had spoken to her weeks ago: *"God brought you to us for a reason, and I'm thanking Him for it every single day."*

I'm thanking You, too, Lord, Christina whispered in her heart. *What You've taken away, You've restored tenfold.*

Epilogue

One Year Later

As Christina and Seth herded the weekend campers toward the Camp Serenity van to head back to San Antonio, nine-year-old Kylie stepped to the side. Backpack tugging at her shoulders, she stretched her arms upward for a hug. "This was the best time of my life. I love you so much, Miss Christina!"

A knot formed in Christina's throat. Casting a misty glance at Seth, she returned the girl's hug. "I love you, too, Kylie, and I'm so glad you could come." Gripping Kylie's shoulders, she looked her squarely in the eye. "And no matter how tough things get at home, keep your chin up—"

"And my eyes on God," Kylie finished with a grin, "because He'll always be with me."

"Exactly." Christina helped the little girl step up into the van. Waving to all the children who'd come to mean so much to her in three short days, she called, "Take care, kids! Hope to see you again soon!"

Greg O'Grady, the driver and one of the weekend chaperones, gave her a grateful nod as she closed the door.

As the van pulled away, she collapsed against Seth and heaved a sigh. "I adore those kids, every single one of them."

Seth brushed her forehead with a light kiss. "You sure made an impression on Kylie. She's a different kid from the scared and angry little girl who arrived here on Friday."

"A lot of that was Gracie's doing. She's still the best dog ever, but she does get a little worn down from all the attention."

"Yep, saw her head to the house with Joseph and Eva earlier. I think we're all ready for a quiet afternoon." Arching a brow, Seth aimed her toward the house. "And you, my dear, need to get off your feet for a while. You were going nonstop all weekend."

"And you weren't? I think we both deserve a spa day." She tucked an arm around her husband's waist, which had much more definition these days than her own.

Inside, Marie and Bethany, a Camp Serenity worker, had just finished loading the dishwasher. "That'll do it," Marie told the girl, one of four college students who'd been hired by Greg's organization to help during these camper retreats. "Why don't you give Tyler and Kate a hand cleaning cabins, and then y'all can take off when you're done."

Seth poured two glasses of his grandmother's raspberry iced tea and handed one to Christina. "Where are the kids?"

"Watching a DVD with Opi and Gracie." Tossing a dish towel onto the counter, Marie blew a damp wisp of hair off her forehead. "And I'm about to join them. Y'all interested?"

Christina shared a knowing look with Seth. Keeping

ten campers and five chaperones fed and entertained all weekend, they'd hardly had a moment to themselves, and Christina was sorely in need of some alone time with her sweetheart. "Maybe in a bit. I need to stretch out for a while."

"Good idea, hon." With an understanding smile, Marie ambled down the hall toward the family room.

In the sitting area of their upstairs suite, Seth plumped the sofa pillows, then helped Christina kick off her sneakers and get comfortable. She was only five months pregnant, but carrying twins, she already felt as big as a house.

Seth sat at the other end of the sofa and pulled her bare feet into his lap for a foot massage. "This'll have to do until you get that spa day."

"It'll do just fine." She sighed with contentment and closed her eyes.

Oh, what a year it had been. About this time last year, Seth and the kids had traveled with her to Little Rock. The weeklong visit gave her parents a chance to get to know Seth, and the affection was mutual from the start.

Christina had also scheduled a meeting with her doctor. Bless his heart, Seth hadn't so much as flinched as the doctor explained in detail the physical and emotional trauma Christina had suffered in the accident and what long-term effects they should expect.

Neither of them cared for the idea of a long engagement, so they set the wedding date for Thanksgiving weekend and held it right here at Serenity Hills. It was a small outdoor wedding by the lake, with family and a few close friends in attendance. And Gracie, of course. Christina's sweet, loyal service dog, adorned in a pouf of white tulle and tiny silk bluebonnets, walked her down the aisle along with her father.

She could still picture her handsome groom in his Western-style tux and polished black cowboy boots. Joseph and Eva stood on either side of him, all of them grinning like they'd just won the biggest prize in the history of the world.

Christina felt exactly the same way about them.

Then, with Gracie sitting between her and Seth, and his two precious children flanking them, they'd recited their vows. They were a family now, and Christina was happier than she'd ever dreamed possible.

When Seth tickled the bottom of her foot, she jerked her eyes open. "What's that big smile about, Mrs. Austin?"

"What it always is." Sitting up, she snuggled beneath his arm. "Remembering our wedding day and counting my blessings."

"Four more months and we'll get to meet our newest blessings." With a hand cupped around his mouth, Seth leaned close to Christina's belly. "Hey in there, your mommy and daddy love you."

A shiver of delight rippled through Christina. After the accident, she had wondered if she'd ever experience the joy of true love, much less the chance to be a mother. But though one disastrous day had changed her life forever, God had always been in control. He'd brought her to Serenity Hills and opened up a whole new future for her, one she could never have planned on her own.

The door creaked open, and two blond heads appeared—three, if Christina counted Gracie, who loved hanging out with the kids these days but was never far away when Christina needed her.

"Hey, Mom and Dad," Joseph greeted with an impish grin. "The movie's over, and Opi said to ask if y'all wanted to go into town for ice cream."

"Oh, he did, did he?" Seth chuckled. "Naturally, y'all had nothing to do with planting the idea in his head."

Shoving past her brother, Eva plowed between Christina and Seth. "Please, Daddy, can we?"

"It's up to your mom." He wiggled a brow at Christina.

Warmth engulfed her at the sound of those sweet words. "Ice cream sounds wonderful—let's go!"

* * * * *

If you loved this tale of sweet romance,
pick up this other story
from author Myra Johnson

RANCHER FOR THE HOLIDAYS

Available now from Love Inspired!

Find more great reads at www.LoveInspired.com

Dear Reader,

Though my husband and I left Texas several years ago to be closer to our grandchildren, as a native Texan with Hill Country family connections, I truly enjoyed this fictional return to my roots. Naturally, the story required a handsome cowboy, and what better setting than a friendly small town and a guest ranch with horses?

Of course, every good story must have conflict, and Christina and her service dog provided exactly what it would take for Seth to change his overprotective mindset and release the fears that held him back from falling in love again. But Christina also had some growing to do. Before she could open her heart to love, she first had to come to full acceptance of both her strengths and her limitations.

Maybe you're facing a situation in which you feel afraid, inadequate or even defeated. If so, remember the Lord's words to Joshua: "Have I not commanded you? Be strong and courageous. Do not be afraid; do not be discouraged, for the Lord your God will be with you wherever you go" (Joshua 1:9, NIV). We are not alone in our struggles. Even when everything seems to conspire against us, we can carry on in faith, knowing that God has already won the ultimate victory.

Thank you for joining me for Seth and Christina's story. I love to hear from readers, so please contact me through my website, www.MyraJohnson.com, or write to me c/o Love Inspired Books, 195 Broadway, New York, NY 10007.

With blessings and gratitude,
Myra

Get 2 Free Books,
Plus 2 Free Gifts—
just for trying the Reader Service!

LI17R2

When an accident strands pregnant widow Willa Chase and her twins at the home of John Miller, she doesn't know if she'll make it back to her Amish community for Christmas. But the reclusive widower soon finds himself hoping for a second chance at family.

Read on for a sneak peek of
AMISH CHRISTMAS TWINS by USA TODAY
bestselling author **Patricia Davids**,
the first in the three-book **CHRISTMAS TWINS** series.

John waited beside Samuel's sleigh and tried unsuccessfully to curb his excitement. He was almost as giddy as Megan and Lucy. A sleigh ride with Willa at his side was his idea of the perfect winter evening, especially since he didn't have to drive. Lucy was the first one out of the house. She quickly claimed her spot in the front seat beside Samuel. Megan came out next and scrambled up beside her sister. He'd never seen the twins so delighted.

Willa took John's hand as he helped her in. He gave her gloved fingers a quick squeeze and saw her smile before she looked down.

Samuel slapped the lines and the big horse took off down the snow-covered lane. Sleigh bells jingled merrily in time with the horse's footfalls, and Megan and Lucy tried to catch snowflakes on their tongues between giggles.

John leaned down to see Willa's face. "Are you warm

enough?" She nodded, but her cheeks looked rosy and cold. John took off his woolen scarf and wrapped it around her head to cover her mouth and nose.

"Danki," she murmured.

"Don't mention it. In spite of the cold, it's a lovely evening to go caroling, isn't it?" The thick snow obscured the horizon and made it feel as if they were riding inside a glass snow globe. The fields lay hidden under a thick blanket of white. A hushed stillness filled the air, broken only by the jingle of the harness bells and the muffled thudding of the horse's feet.

Their first destination was only a mile from John's house. As Lucy and Megan scrambled down from the sleigh, John offered Willa his hand to help her out.

"Was this what you imagined Christmas would be like when you decided to return to your Amish family?"

She shook her head. "I never imagined anything like this. Do you do it every year?"

"We do."

"You aren't going to actually sing, are you, John?"

He threw back his head and laughed. *"Nee*, but I will hum along."

"Softly, dear, softly," she suggested.

He wondered if she realized that she had called him "dear." It was turning out to be an even more wonderful night than he had hoped for.

Don't miss
AMISH CHRISTMAS TWINS
by Patricia Davids, available October 2017 wherever
Love Inspired® books and ebooks are sold.

www.LoveInspired.com

Inspirational Romance to
Warm Your Heart and Soul

Join our social communities to connect
with other readers who share your love!

Sign up for the Love Inspired newsletter
at **www.LoveInspired.com** to be the
first to find out about upcoming titles,
special promotions and exclusive content.

CONNECT WITH US AT:

Harlequin.com/Community

 Facebook.com/LoveInspiredBooks

 Twitter.com/LoveInspiredBks

LISOCIAL2017